Bitter COLD Holiday

J.K. Rohde

To Sandy
Keep warm in the
U.P.! ~ Jim

JKRohde

This is a work of fiction. All characters portrayed in this novel are either fictitious or are used fictitiously.

Wishingstone Woods
Publishing
P.O. Box 444,
Iron River, MI 49935

ISBN-13: 978-1481981057
ISBN-10: 1481981056

Dedicated to my mom,
Lois Gunderman,
who gave to me the love
of reading and writing;
and shared with me
her Lake Superior.

❖❖ **1** ❖❖

Come join us, come join us...

It was as if the snow squalls, flirting across Lake Superior, were summoning us to participate in their impassioned dance. If the northern lights of summer could be called spirit dancers, these apparitions of winter should have been cast as specters in an ice ballet. Their performance was beautifully dangerous. We were inside and not beckoning their call; not yet anyway.

The soft rhythms of Yuletide music continued to play as birch logs crackled in the fireplace. Flames licked into the air warning us to ignore the unrelenting gales. The fire's warmth was reassuring against the torrents of the great, white north. Still, it held its own menace as if laughing at us, offering a false sense of security.

A freshly cut spruce sat in the corner of my cabin with its tiny lights tiptoeing across silver tinsel. Candle lanterns filtered diamond shapes onto the log walls. Hollyberries ringed a bowl of tempting chocolates. It was very romantic. The only thing missing were the men. It was just us girls - Della, Cricket and me, Lexi Marx – three women, trying to keep warm on a cold, winter night.

We were bundled in woolen slippers and old, quilted blankets. Cups of mulled wine warming our hands as the forces of Gitchi-Gummi rattled the frail window panes. Jack Frost and Father Christmas were battling for their right to enter and entertain us. They had a few weeks to sort it out. I was hoping Frost would loose. It may have been wishful thinking.

Cricket, my irreplaceable friend, was more interested in the cookies than the howling cold.

Della kept an eye on the north window as she huddled tightly under her blanket, "I haven't been up here in the winter since I was a kid. How do you deal with it day after day?"

"It's just wind," Cricket said through a mouth full of sugar, "and a little ice, some snow and cold. It's no big deal, for me anyway. I have a lot of insulation." She patted her thigh.

"But Lexi probably has on ten pairs of thermals," she eyed me over the chocolates, "She needs to put some sugar on her bones if she's going to keep from freezing to death."

"I've only got on three pairs of long johns, and two tops, and okay, two wool sweaters," I said while huddling closer to the fireplace.

Della laughed, "And you're shivering. I can understand why I'm freezing. I'm getting up there in age, at a whopping forty-four, but you are so young."

"At thirty-one, I'm in between youthful romps in the snow and having leathered my skin to the weather." An involuntary quiver trickled down my spine.

Turning from the fire, I followed Della's gaze out past the cabin window to the woods beyond, where a spire rose above the snow scalloped tree line.

"The wind is always rattling and scratching. It makes the cats crazy," I said, "and I get spooked. But we love it here. You came during a storm. Wait until the sun shines. It is beautiful."

"Speaking of spooks," Cricket said between cookie crumbs, "I heard the kids in town say that they saw a ghost in the old lodge last week."

She latched onto the bowl of popcorn and quickly stuffed her mouth full. It reminded me of the little chipmunk that visits my back porch in the summer. I could tell she was trying to divert herself from chattering. Della, who had turned her gaze toward the fire, mesmerized by the continuous motion of the flames, darted a look at Cricket. For the first time since she arrived, earlier in the day, her grief-weary eyes began to brighten. "What are you saying?"

"Who said they saw a ghost?" I asked.

Cricket explained that her fourteen year old sister, Jana, had heard the other kids at school talking about it. While snowmobiling along the lakeshore, the kids saw a bluish light moving through the estate house. I reminded Cricket that even though she loved a good ghost story, *they*, meaning spooks or apparitions, didn't need to use a light.

Cricket looked at me with her big brown eyes and said, "Lexi, I know that, but *they* weren't using a light, *they* were the light."

Della had returned to a distant world deep within the captivating fire. With a whisper as soft as a falling snowflake she said, "I wish it was my dad's spirit roaming through the big house. I'd like to see him again."

She turned her now watery eyes from the hypnotic flames back toward her family lodge that lay beyond the window and said, "I image it's true of anyone who has just lost someone dear to them. We miss them desperately. That's why I came up here. After the funeral, all I wanted was to be in Ottawa. We had good memories from summer vacations at the estate. Being along the big lake makes me feel closer to him. I thought maybe it would make the ache go away, just a little."

"I'm so sorry about your dad," Cricket leaned away from the empty bowl. "Lexi told me that he was old, but that you still took it hard."

Della nodded. I could see that she was remembering the days she had spent in this little town of Ottawa with her family. The True family was legendary here. And Della B. True was part of that history. Tucking her cardigan over her shoulders, I inched my toes closer to the hearth and stretched my lower limbs across the weathered rug. Its faded braids barely cushioned my body from the wood floor. The threadbare carpet still served its purpose by keeping the chill from seeping up from the foundation, or lack of it. My northwoods cottage-home was not built for a northern winter.

Della pulled her knees up to her chest and rested her chin on them and said, "My dad loved this cabin the best of those he'd built for his guests. I remember, when I was a kid, we'd sneak over here from the lodge at sunset, so that he could smoke his pipe. We'd stare out that window, looking out over Lake Superior, and he'd tell me stories about the ships he'd built. *'Some made great journeys,'* he'd say, *'while others met with their ruin during terrible storms that came without warning on that big lake.'* I'll miss our talks."

"I wish I would have met him," I said, imagining his big ships crossing Lake Superior.

"Maybe you can," Cricket piped in.

"What do you mean?" I asked.

Della and I stared at Cricket. Her eyes began to sparkle like a Christmas icicle and she said, "What about that ghost? Is anyone up for an adventure?"

Neither the cold of night nor meeting ghosts of dads-past held a glimmer of appeal for me. I opened my mouth to protest when Della said, "We *could* go check it out."

She turned toward me. Her familiar closed mouth smile and glinting hazel-brown eyes were about six inches from my face. I knew that tonight I'd be out leathering my thin skin, in that blasted cold, on an icy escapade. Cricket popped off the sofa sending my already traumatized cat, Pixie, sprinting from the room. I'm not sure if it was the upset cat that yowled or my excited friend, but either way the sound made us laugh.

Cricket offered Della and me a hand up from the floor. We exchanged our cozy slippers for heavy winter boots. We tucked arms into down parkas before tugging on hats, scarves and mittens.

"Lexi, do you have flashlights?" Cricket asked. I nodded, plucked off the mittens, plodded off to the kitchen and dug through the junk drawer, always the largest drawer in the kitchen, returning with three mismatched lights of various sizes. I kept the smallest one. I preferred it. It could be held between my teeth if I needed both hands for hauling wood, grabbing cats or, most importantly, using the *outdoor facilities;* the woods.

Before repositioning my mitts, I snuffed the candles and placed the grate in front of the fireplace. I could feel the tapping of Cricket's boot vibrating through the floorboards.

"Getting overheated here," said Cricket, jiggling the brass door knob, "I have too many layers, even without the parka. Are you ready?"

* * *

Even with all five layers of clothing, my hat pulled down to my eyebrows and my scarf wrapped up to my eyelashes, it was frightfully cold. The wind pushed the chill of winter right through the weave of my jeans and layers of thermal underwear. Instantly, I felt it chafe my thighs. Cricket straightened her five foot one inch frame, tipped her head up directly into the iced air, which seemed to always accompany the winter wind off Superior, and trotted down the narrow path that lead to *True North*, Della's family estate.

Della leaned into me as if we could fend off the weather and create extra warmth if we stuck tight to each other. A tune was reeling through my head, *Oh the weather outside is frightful...*

I could hear Cricket whistling, *Let it snow, let it snow let it snow...* I had to smile, and could feel Della laugh. "Is it the snow, or the fact that she's getting to do something exciting, that has her acting so bubbly?" Della asked.

"Actually," I said, "I think it's the ghost."

Cricket was waiting by the side entrance for us to make our way through one final snow drift. "Good thing we know our way and didn't have to follow your lead," I said to Cricket while stomping snow off my boots, "Your tracks nearly filled in before you stepped out of them."

"Wicked out tonight," Della said while locating the key from behind a loose piece of chinking in a log. "It's still where my dad left it." She wiggled the skeleton key in the lock a few times before it clicked into place. Turning the knob she stopped.

"What's wrong?" Cricket whispered.

"Nothing," Della paused and then pushed the door farther. The wood creaked from the cold, and then it stuck. "It's that old throw rug. It always bunched up and caught the door. I'll squeeze through and move it." As she wriggled in through the slim opening, I could feel the heat of adrenaline spilling through me, even though I was shivering from the cold. From one foot to the next, I rocked and shifted, and waited.

"Della?" Cricket said, "Let us in."

I stopped fidgeting, and listened. I could hear creaking boards, off to the left of the door, inside the building. Then they'd stop. There was a rustling of what sounded like paper. Then there was more creaking boards.

"What is she doing?" Cricket asked, "Why isn't she letting us in?"

"Sshhh, I'm listening," I told her and pressed my ear closer to the door just as it opened wide.

Cricket snatched my arm and wedged us through the opening, "Thought maybe you wanted friend-sicles for a snack tonight." She began shining her light around the room and into the adjoining kitchen.

"I just needed a minute to myself," Della said.

Cricket nodded as she left the confines of the small entry and stepped onto the worn linoleum of the lodge's kitchen. Again, Della and I locked shoulders and stepped into the dark room. Dust particles were frozen in mid air. Behind the stillness of the closed-up building the wind snagged at window panes and shifted the shingles on the roof. The cold was lying heavy on top of wooden sideboards and discolored countertops. The butcher's block was weighted with not only dull unmoving air, but also with knives and the stains from many past meals of venison steak, freshly caught fish, homegrown potatoes, rutabagas and squash. As our lights glanced from surface to surface a picture was beginning to take shape. It was minus the details, but *True North* once coffered a wealth of living.

As we moved into the dining room, with its long oak table, Della ran her mitten covered hand across the dark wood and looked down at it. "It was my job to set the table for dinner," she said smiling. Then her expression changed and she frowned, "My sister Moira would whine that '*she wanted to do it*', so I'd let her and I'd go off to read. When it came time to eat, mom would bring out the food and she'd start to scold me '*I thought I told you to set the table?*' Moira would stand behind her and smile devilishly at me. I never tattled on her. Instead, I'd blame it on the book I was reading. I'd give her another chance every week, hoping that maybe she'd actually do the chore. She never did. But, I got smarter and beat mama to the table. Moira was a conniving child, and has grown into an even worse adult. "

She looked up from the table, "I could go on with stories all night, but we'd freeze." She rubbed her hands together and said, "See any ghosts yet Cricket?"

"I've been looking, but there's nothing spooky here," she said aiming her flashlight above the fireplace mantel, "Except maybe that glassy-eyed deer head." As we stared up at the ant-lered deer mount, a gust of air cut through the frozen confines of the dining room. It hooked around us, as if drawing our steps forward. Each of our flashlight beams floated warily toward the arched doorway to the main room which faced Lake Superior.

"Open window?" I muttered, searching for a reasonable explanation.

"Ghost?" said Cricket with more cheer than fear in her voice.

Della was the first to succumb to the beckoning current of cold as it lead her through the log archway into the great room. Her flashlight beam cut through the dust as she aimed for her father's den at the far side of the lodge. I glanced at Cricket. We followed in Della's footsteps, literally, the dust left better tracks than the snow had earlier.

She was standing in front of the den's fireplace. As we entered the room she turned toward us, "It's coming from here. Maybe the damper let loose or came open?"

There was a clatter of metal against brick deep inside the chimney, then it stopped and so did the stream of cold air. Papers had been scattered on the floor near a black walnut desk. Della bent down and started pawing at the papers trying to snatch them between thumb and mitten tips. Finally she removed the bulky mitts and piled each paper carefully atop the next.

"I don't want anything disturbed," she said, "It'll be fuel for Moira's fire, or any of the other relatives coming to Ottawa with hopes of putting *True North* under their Christmas tree."

She smoothed the papers, looked up at us and said, "I'm the only one who ever came back, since we were kids. I'm the only one who cared about this place after our parents got old, or passed away. My dad was the last. I should have kept it up better, cleaned it and fixed the windows and chimneys."

Her eyes were getting watery again; she turned toward Lake Superior which lay beyond the pinerow and juniper bushes outside the frosty windows, "I'm so sorry dad. I miss you, *True North* misses you."

Clanking resumed inside the chimney flue, it rattled as if a train were coursing down through the bricks. A gust of wind sent a sooty, black ball of smoky tar and creosote into the room with a puff. It rose toward the ceiling and hung in mid air, frozen. The damper clanked even harder and shattered down onto the wrought iron grate. As it hit iron and ash it sounded like noises from a one-man-band: clink-clatter-clatter-poof. The ball of soot continued to hover like a black, translucent snowball. We edged back closer to the wall. Our flashlights had moved up toward the black orb, and then down to the ashes and back again to the strange, filmy sphere holding us captivated in the book lined den. Cricket broke the silence, "I smell trouble."

A bright light shot across the floor and walls of the adjoining great room. We froze. The intense white light was unnaturally intrusive to the darkened lodge. Dust particles hung like an eerie crystallized curtain, heightening our already over stimulated imaginations.

Della was the first to thaw to a logical reaction.

"Shut off your lights," she said.

"Why?" Cricket asked, still gelid in the moment.

"It's a car," I said, panic heating my cryogen brain into clearer thinking. We were all whispering. We didn't move. I glanced up. The ghostly black ball of icy soot was gone.

Della said quietly, "Let's go this way. Just stay close to the wall so we don't cast any shadows." We followed her out of the den, around the corner, through a long hallway and out onto a side deck. By the time we made it through the darkened building to the outside, our visitor was merely two red taillights receding through the shadowy thicket of trees. Breaths of relief were exhaled in steaming puffs.

I said, "Let's go back to the cabin." We started around the front corner of the lodge.

As I clicked on my flashlight, its beam, which should have spread out across the snowy lawn, was instantly focused on the face of a person only a foot in front of me. The light reflecting off a pair of eye glasses gave the appearance of a ghastly wild eyed beast. I screamed, which caused a chain reaction from Della and Cricket. I also tripped, forward unfortunately, toward the horrifying image, and tried to regain my footing without luck. My arm flew up. My flashlight hit the creature and we toppled into the snow. I started swinging my arms and kicking my legs while trying to push myself up. Snow does not offer leverage. I kept sinking in. I had lost my hat and one mitten. The snow was drenching my face and burning my checks. I was breathing hard.

Finally I heard Cricket's voice yelling over the wind, "Lexi stop moving; it's okay."

In the dark, I could make out her shape above me, along with Della's and a taller slimmer form beside her. He was laughing.

Cricket's flashlight then blinded me, "Get that out of my eyes, I can't see."

The taller form, which was still laughing, stepped forward and reached out a helping hand, and said, "You'd have gotten up faster if you hadn't been wrestling so hard with yourself."

Grabbing the outstretched hand I righted myself, and said, "Why did you sneak up on me like that? And what are you doing out here?"

Foster Keene smiled as he brushed snow off my jacket and pants, found my mitten and hat. He began to explain that a couple kids told the sheriff that someone was messing around at the estate. His explanation was being seized by the voice of the lake wind, "We thought... vandals... rode ... sheriff...check it out."

"What?" Cricket said.

"Let's get back to the cabin," I barked, "I'm freezing."

The wind was sharp. We faced into the icy air. Cricket kept close, trying to ask questions, offer theories and out shout Mother Nature. Finally, Della smacked the top of her head with a mittened hand and told her to keep it down until we were inside. I think she said the trees have ears, but Boreas, the north wind, may have frozen mine by then.

* * *

After shedding all my outdoor apparel, I hurried to the bathroom. When I returned to the cabin's living room Foster was stoking the fire. Della was putting on water for something – anything - hot. Cricket was scavenging the cupboards.

"So, Foster, tell us again what you were doing at *True North* tonight?" Della said with a raised brow while filling cups. She placed each of the steaming mugs on the table, grabbed a basket filled with packets of tea, cider, cocoa and flavored coffees, and then looked at the young journalist-photographer who was still poking at the burning logs. I was helping Cricket fill a tray with crackers, cheeses, sausage and cookies.

Foster waited until we were all in one room. He continued rearranging the hot embers, making the logs snap and sizzle, as he began his story again. "Like I said, Judd had heard from some kids that there was someone messing around out at the big place, so I rode with him to check it out. I looked in the window and saw that it was the three of you, so the sheriff headed back to town."

"And you stayed?" Cricket asked.

He reached a long arm over to the coffee table, latched on-to a cookie, and said, "Well sure, I was curious. That's my job you know."

"I don't see a camera or notebook Mr. Newsguy," Cricket teased, then looked at me with a questioning look. *What? I looked back at her.* She tipped her head for me to follow her into the kitchen. We excused ourselves with the ruse of scavenging for more cookies.

Once in the kitchen she said, "Can we talk about what we saw at the lodge in front of Foster?"

"It's okay with me," Della said from the other room, "It's a small cabin, we can hear you."

Cricket grabbed more cookies, some of my mom's pizzellis and a mug of hot cocoa. Reclaiming her spot on the sofa, she told Foster the whole story.

Della added bits of information, or gently corrected her exaggerations. "Obviously, Cricket thinks it was a ghost," she said to Foster.

"What do you think it was?" he asked her.

"Logically, it could very well have been caused from the cold and moisture, but not realistically. It was just hovering there. Lexi, do you remember seeing anything else."

I shook my head, looked at Della and said, "I think it would be great if it was your dad. I understand. I still miss my Nana, and it's been over three years since she died. There's been so many times that I've wished she was alive to help me understand things."

The events of the night, extra exertion and the snug warmth of the cabin lulled us into nostalgia. My tiger striped cat, Pan, walked across my lap and began pawing at my sweater. Cricket was scratching the ears of Pan's twin sister, Pixie.

Della laid a hand on my arm and said, "I remember the first summer that I met your Nana. She must have known that she wouldn't be around much longer and asked me to look after you. I guess I had that motherly look to me.

"That was when she explained to me about the unique *gift* the two of you shared. At first I thought she was old and senile. I humored her. At eighty-seven, she was quite sharp and could see I was skeptical. She had me show her the contents of my purse. She pointed at my little red stain pouch. I handed it to her. She held it and began to explain to me exactly where I had been and what I had been thinking the last time I had held the pouch. It was amazing."

"You never told me that before," I said to her.

Cricket quickly asked, "What did she see?"

Della smiled up at us, "She told me that I had been looking out over Lake Superior, thinking about my Joe. It was the second anniversary of his death. I was thinking of how he'd been lost during that terrible storm, and that I missed him desperately." She paused, and then added, "I was still a little uncertain about what she was saying, and then, your Nana smiled at me and said that my pouch held four wild rose petals. Joe had given them to me before he had left on that fishing trip. One petal stood for me, two were for our children; and the fourth was for our grandson. I had been remembering how Joe had kissed me and told me the petals represented everything he loved. After hearing her repeat to me what I had experienced, I was a believer. No one could have known that."

Della wrapped an arm around me, gently brushing static filled strands of my coffee-brown hair away from my teary eyes, and said, "I promised her that I would always believe you."

I laid my head against her shoulder while thinking about my grandmother and great grandmother and many more of the old-European women who had kept our family secret; sharing it with only a few close friends. It was a hard secret to hide. Ever since my early teens, I'd been able to know things.

As if reading my mind, Cricket began rambling about all the trouble I'd gotten into in school because I could see who the mischief-makers were after they had spray painted walls, stopped up bathroom sinks or dabbled in an assortment of other pranks. Teachers would always accuse me of being involved in the damage. Finally, I learned to keep quiet.

Foster had continued to poke at the fire while we had our little walk down memory lane. He looked up at me and said, "You could get out the *Stones* and see if they can help us sort out this ghost thing."

Della nodded, the cat meowed and Cricket reached up onto the wooden bookcase and lifted down my Nana's velvet blue pouch which held her *Sorting Stones*.

Taking the pouch reminded me of my Nana who taught me how to use the unique gifts I now possessed. Cricket's family comforted the masses with food. Foster came from a long line of newspaper people and writers. Della's family had impacted the world by building ships and beautiful homes. Mine touched it in a different way.

I poured the smooth white stones into my palm. Della, Cricket and Foster all knew the story of the *Stones*. They had been gathered along the beaches of Lake Superior. Nana would roll them in her hands to help sort out her thoughts, including the time my granddad asked her to marry him. She had sorted and sorted the stones until she had one stone left in her hand, the right stone for her, and the right man to call her husband. She kept that smooth, white stone from the pouch and had it made into a heart shaped pendant which she wore faithfully every day. The white agate heart was also passed on to me.

As I thought of my Nana and Della's father, I rolled the stones in my hands. Their cool, hard surfaces were beginning to warm. I laid them on the braided rug in front of the fireplace. Foster had the fire roaring and the flames cast colored patterns onto their white surfaces. I moved the stones around, first into a circle then one by one moved each into a different position. After a few moments of repositioning, Della gasped, "Don't touch them! Look, do you see it?"

Moving my head, tipping it back and forth, I saw it. There were eyes, nose and a mouth; a man's facial features were distinctly visible. I looked up at Della, she was staring at it. "It's my dad's face."

As the flames danced around, the shadows shifted, and the image became distorted, angry, then, smiling.

"It *was* him at the big house," Cricket said, "I knew it." She slapped her leg, and the cat jumped right into the stones, scattering them across the rug.

"Sorry," Cricket said as she looked over at the late Carsen True's daughter, whose eyes were tearing for the loss of her beloved father.

I had seen something else. It had escaped the others gathered around the *Sorting Stones*. Reflected on the rock's surfaces, I saw a storm as black as burnt, charred logs. Fiery, red eyes sparked with hatred. Gold coins being grabbed at by hot, orange fingers. The wickedly cold implications made me shiver.

◆◆ **2** ◆◆

Just hear those sleigh bells ring-a-ling, ting, ting, ting-a-ling...

Peter Holloway looked up from soaking his breakfast in maple syrup as Della, Cricket and I walked into the Shipwreck Café. The familiar chiming of the captain's bell on the door was replaced with a sleigh bell for the holiday season. As in most small towns, when the front door of the local café opens, heads lift and turn. Ottawa wasn't any different. Everyone wants to see who the tide brought in, or during the winter months, who blew in on the tail of the blizzard.

Peter stood and said, "Della B. True, what brings you to Ottawa at this time of year?"

She walked over to him, held out her arms from under her green, woolen cape to welcome the man who over the years had doggedly vied for her affections. They kissed each other on the cheek in a friendly embrace.

"Good morning Mr. Holloway," then turning to his breakfast companion, "and to you Sheriff Judd Golden." It was a pleasure watching Della. She had a way of turning a room from ordinary to brilliant. "I've come to check on *True North,*" she said while looking at Judd. Untying her wide-brimmed, felted hat, wrapped securely in a woolen scarf, she continued, "My dear dad, who I don't believe either of you had the good fortune to meet, decided it was his time to be called to the big ship yard beyond." She looked at Peter and smiled, "You'd have liked him."

"If he was anything like his daughter, I believe I would have."

Mabel, who owned the Shipwreck Café, and her grand-niece Allisa, moved another table up against Peter and Judd's to accommodate the three of us, while Christmas music played old time favorites.

"I remember your papa," Mabel said, "and your mama too; good people. They would come up in the summer and throw the biggest parties Ottawa ever saw." She positioned chairs and passed out menus. "He'd invite the whole town over to the lodge for barbeques and fireworks. Sorry to hear he's gone." She patted Della's shoulder and then was hailed by Herb's call from the kitchen, *'Order's up!'*

Her grand-niece poured coffee and set an extra plate for Foster who jingled into our morning reunion. Allisa, at sixteen, was donning a smile on Foster, as she said "The special today is the *Peninsula*. It's berries-of-the-north, mixed with a sweet cream cheese filling, tucked into Uncle Herb's home-made French toast, and topped with fresh whipped cream. It's really good. I'll be right back."

As she left the table, Judd asked Foster, "So, were they causing any trouble at the big house last night?"

"Nope, but I nearly got knocked out with a flashlight. Good thing Lexi wields a mini Mag-light." He said while making a swashbuckling motion.

My cheeks went warm, but I'm not sure if it was from embarrassment or windburn. Cricket was quiet as she read the menu, then said, "Peter, have you ever seen chimney soot freeze in mid-air?" I kicked her under the table. She winced, but recovered nicely, "I mean can soot blow down out of a frozen chimney?"

He eyed her suspiciously, but then dropped the inquiring look. He probably thought, like the rest of us, that Cricket was always full of odd questions, as he answered, "Old chimneys are usually full of soot, maybe even bats or squirrels."

"I think the damper broke in the den fireplace at *True North*," Della added.

"I could take a look at it if you'd like?" he said politely. He was showing his manners, as was Judd, by waiting for us to order before continuing with their breakfasts.

Della noticed the plate of maple syrup soaked French toast and hash browns, "We didn't mean to interrupt your breakfast, please eat while it's still warm, we're glad to have hot coffee. It sure is cold this year."

"Actually," Foster began, primed to give a newscaster's account of weather conditions, "Last night, there was an unusual amount of moisture in the air."

I chose to interject a more artistic account, "The icy blasts off the lake had felt crystallized. It was bitter cold."

The sleigh bell jingled and we turned to see what could have been described as the anti-Santa. She was dressed all in black from her head to her foot, and her face was pale and tight. She scanned the café. Riveting eyes froze on Della. She stalked straight to our table.

"Hello, Moira," Della said in a smooth unruffled tone.

She flipped back her heavy black wool cape, nearly identical to her sister's, except for the malevolence which drifted out from under it.

"Well sister, I see you've beaten me to the treasure. It figures. How are things at the big house? Are the brass candlesticks still in residence or have they disappeared, too?"

"Yes, I've been there, and all is as it was. Would you like to join us for breakfast? These are my friends Lexi Marx, Foster Keene, *Sheriff* (she emphasized sheriff) Judd Golden and Peter Holloway."

Moira opened her sneering, red lips to speak. As her eyes followed around the table and ended on the rugged woodsman, seated next to the sheriff, she closed her mouth and issued a deliberate smile. "Peter, it's nice to meet you. I'm Moira B. True." Peter had set down his fork, again. His food had to be as cold as the icy woman that stood over him.

Della cleared her throat in agitation, something I've never heard her do, and said, "Moira, are you staying in Ottawa?"

With implacably sharp eyes, Della's sister stared at her, "Yes I am; at *True North.*"

Della, obviously flustered and peeved, stood to face her sister straightly, nose to nose. They were the same height, with the same squared shoulders above thinly built, five-foot eight-inch frames. Their strong features and high cheek-boned faces could have been a mirrored image except for the laugh lines which Moira lacked.

"You can't," Della said.

"Yes, I can."

"I mean, you can't because there isn't any heat, water or electricity."

Moira paused, tapped her fingernail on the table. She turned, "Peter? Would you be able to help me, with *True North*? I'm sure a man like you knows how to do all those things," she said waiving a fluttery hand toward Della and her fix-up list for the estate house.

Peter laid down his fork again, wiped his mouth and in all honesty I thought he was going to scold her like an unruly, rude child. Instead he said, "That, m'am, is my occupation and I'd be glad to be hired to get the True sisters' home ready for the holidays."

Moira twitched. First her eyes, then her head, then her hand, then her foot. "Thank you. That would be nice," she said in a strained voice, "and would you be able to start today."

"I can," Peter replied, "and it should be ready for inspection in three days."

"Oh, Peter, I'll be inspecting it everyday, more than once." She turned, rewrapped her cape in a sweeping motion, and strode rigidly from the cafe. We stared after her as her black form contrasted against the pure white snow blanketing Ottawa.

"I think she looks like a big, black bug," Foster said.

"Hey, don't go giving us bugs a bad name," Cricket said, defending her nickname and her birth name - Christina Bugsby.

Della sat down, "I think I've lost my appetite. I knew she'd come, but I'd forgotten how awful she can be. I don't know if I can ..." She stopped, looked around, and more in character, apologized and ordered the *Peninsula*.

I'll be home for Christmas played softly in the background.

Peter broke the uncomfortable silence at the table, "If you'd like, maybe we could go over to the lodge and you could show me what you think needs to be done?"

She smiled softly and said, "Thank you. I would like to start doing some renovations. It's beautiful under all the dust that's accumulated over years of neglect. I should have done it sooner."

"I can help too," I said, "if you want? I'm finished with my last commissioned art piece for the year, and other than getting the decorations ready for Holly Fest, my schedule's open."

"Thanks, Lexi, I'd love your help."

Peter had sopped up his last bit of syrup, wiped his napkin down over his trim, silvering beard and with an alluring southern drawl he'd acquired from the majority of his life spent in Tennessee, he said, "Miss Della, don't you worry. We'll get the old place spruced up for you. Winter in Ottawa is the best time to do a project like that, not much else happening 'round here."

On cue, Judd's radio crackled to life, "Sheriff, you there?" It was the deputy's voice. "We've got a car in the ditch out here on the Red Earth Road, a sporty little red one, with a driver so lively and quick tongued, we knew in a moment it couldn't be St. Nick." Everyone laughed at the 'tis the season rhetoric by the deputy. "She's spouting all kinds of nasty little words about this *God forsaken place and meeting her family,* and we can't get a straight answer out of the little blonde racer. Maybe she bumped her head or something. Any suggestions?"

"Get a tow truck and bring her in here. Maybe she'll calm down a little," the sheriff instructed. Looking at Peter he said, "What was that you said about nothing happening?"

Peter laughed. Della, on the other hand, let out an audible sigh accompanied by only one word, "Trudi."

◆◆ **3** ◆◆

Where the treetops glisten…

There are times when my bright yellow Explorer is fun and exciting, and then there are times like this when it stands out like a Hawaiian prom dress at a funeral. I was pulling up to the winter castle of *True North* in a big banana instead of a charming horse drawn sleigh. It did not fit in with the picturesque logs and stone of the lodge set in the fairy like wonderland of pines, along Lake Superior's pristine shoreline. *The next time I go vehicle shopping I'm leaving Cricket home,* I thought.

Della's silver Navigator fit the scene to a tee, sleek and stunning. Even Peter's old blue work truck was less obtrusive than my big Bahaman-buggy. With the driveway plowed and the walkways shoveled the place looked more inviting than the previous night. Snow drifts lay against the smooth lake stones which wrapped the entire lower third of the lodge. Darkened plank wood, weathered from Superior's harsh winds, covered most of the exterior. The turret, which towered above the angular roof lines, was made entirely of native rock. Tall, thin-paned windows were trimmed in cottage red and amber gold. Ornately carved wooden finials of acorns and oak leaves graced the porch railings. Hand-hewn, northern white cedar logs created the massive great-room which faced the great lake. I breathed in its beauty and imagined how spectacular it would be decked-out for the holidays.

The immense wood door stuck along its arched top as I pushed it forward. It gave way with a loud crack that echoed through the vast spaces both inside and out. A shiver crept under my heavy layers of clothing as the sound continued to reverberate through each room, up the heavy staircase to the second floor which was visible from the foyer. As the noise moved through the expanse of the building and then bounced back off the icy window panes, it gained momentum rather than fading into the ether, at it should have.

I wondered why Della hadn't ever brought me here in the summertime when she had visited Ottawa. The building had always looked omnificent from the beach with its precipitous roof lines reaching toward the skies. It was none the less impressive on the inside. I stepped onto a woven carpet that lay over black and white marble squares, heaved the door shut and called out, "Hello?" The echo came again, so did the shivers. I waited. No answer, so I moved through an arched door frame that opened into the great-room and called again, more softly, "Hello?", still no answer.

Heavy draperies had been pulled back to expose the breathtaking view of the lake. Even frozen over for miles it was awesome. During the light of day, I could see better the lay of the lodge. The dining room area and kitchen were set toward the south of the estate. The den was ahead of me and off to the right. Above, the ceiling of the great-room was beamed with huge, square cut, timberframe logs. The wood was dark with age. I was staring up at the enormous structure and not paying attention to where I was stepping. I tripped and fell against an old cedar chest. My legs twisted under me and a boot heel wedged itself precariously under my backside. Through my mittens I could feel a splinter of wood poking into my palm. I looked around, still no one in sight. The mittens came off, the sliver removed and in the process of getting back up I placed both hands onto the antique, seaman's chest for leverage.

Everything that I had been seeing disappeared within my mind. My sight flashed to summertime at the lodge. The room was filled with women in floral dresses and men in cotton shirts and summer weight trousers. There were the sounds of laughter and talking while the waves rhythmically beat to music, either swing or big band. I could feel myself smiling and warm. I looked down at my feet. They were small, tanned and dotted with sand. My hands looked the same as they jiggled a doll by its arms making it dance to the scratchy tune. My body jerked as a loud crash erupted. It was the breaking of glass. It made me stop the doll from dancing and look out into the room where all the laughing and talking had been replaced with silence. A small girl stood in the middle of the room with shattered glasses by her feet. A woman dressed in a crisp, peach-colored dress and white apron grabbed her arm. I was still smiling and warm as I slid off my spot on the wood chest.

It was gone, all the color and warmth, as quickly as it had appeared. The room was cold and silent. Then, I heard footsteps and talking. I slipped my mittens back on as Della and Peter rounded the corner by the French doors of the den. "Lexi, what happened?" Della said as she hurried to me, reaching down for my hand.

"I tripped."

"Are you alright?"

"Just a bit dizzy."

"Come, sit down. Peter, would you be a dear and bring the thermos from the kitchen?"

She led me to the dining room, where a fire was laboring ineffectively to generate some warmth.

"It could take days to heat this big, old house," Peter said while placing the thermos and cups on the table, "but we're working on it, one fireplace at a time."

"The furnace man will be here shortly," Della added, "but we have electricity, and space heaters. It was probably one of the heater cords that snagged your step."

"This place is amazing," I told her while looking around at the detailed stonework of the fireplace and its carved mantel. The latticed windows were underscored with cushioned seats covered in rich, green brocades depicting hunting scenes. The antique hutches were laden with milky green, Fire King glassware and hand painted tea cups.

"It's also amazing how much work needs to be done to it," she added holding up a clipboard filled with pages of details.

The crack of the wooden front door again began its echo-trail through the lodge followed by a piercing, "The first thing that needs to be fixed is this damn door. Della where are you?"

"Ah, she has arrived. We're in here, Moira."

◆◆ 4 ◆◆

Christmas makes you feel emotional...

The black cape was replaced with a belted black coat. The red lips were still in place, as was the scowl. "Where is the heat? I thought you'd have heat."

Peter stepped in, as general contractor, and said, "The furnace is old, so..."

But, before he could finish she began on a tirade, "Of course it's old, everything here is old from the floor to the roof, which I'm sure will need to be replaced, along with these nasty wood planks that have passed for floors all these years. They are disgusting. New doors, windows, carpets and appliances are in order, too. And look at those curtains, dreadful. I can only imagine how many bugs and things have crawled into the upholstery and mattresses." She swirled around and came face to face with Della, whose cheeks were as hot as the flames in the fireplace.

"Now, Moira," she began, but was interrupted, once again, by that horrid crack of the front door.

"Helll-oooo, Where is everyone?"

"Trudi," Della said and then much louder replied, "We're in here."

The woman who came through the door *was* the Hawaiian prom dress. Hot pink ski jacket was accessorized with multicolored striped scarf and hat, lime green gloves and fur trimmed boots which came from nearly the same green dye lot. She snatched back silky blonde hair while looking into corners as if cobwebs could damage her un-split ends. Della met her by the fireplace and they gave each other a hug, which was more like a pat on the shoulders. As Della turned back toward the door she said, "Beth Ann, I can't believe it's you, it's been years."

The flaccid featured woman patted her graying hair, pulled back into a braided bun, and fidgeted with her woven headband as she stepped toward Della's open arms. "It has been a while, hasn't it? We, Trudi and I, were so sorry to hear about Uncle Carsen; and that we couldn't make it to the funeral."

They all turned to look at Moira, who was beginning again, "My, my, look whose come to pay their respects, and check out their inheritance. That is why you've come isn't it girls?"

"How about you Moira?" said Trudi, still eyeing the crevices in the wood, "Isn't that why you're here? The only ones missing are Blair and Hazel, or are they in the attic playing silly games?"

"We haven't seen them, yet," Della said.

"They may not come, Blair doesn't like to take Hazel out very often," Beth Ann said, now fussing with the slightly worn cuffs of her delft blue, faux fur coat.

Della moved back to the far side of the table and said, pointing toward Peter and me sitting like the audience at the theater, "We, Peter Holloway, our contractor, and my friend Lexi Marx, were going over a list of things the old house needs, because Moira wants to stay here while in Ottawa."

Our theater performance continued. Each of them began talking over the top of the other with questions and accusations. Even Della took part in the verbal wrangling.

Trudi: *Why does she get to stay her? Because she's the oldest?*

Beth Ann: *Maybe we should all stay here? But it's awfully cold.*

Moira: *Don't you have a book club to go to, or ski trip to run off on?*

Trudi: *Better than sitting in the dark plotting against the neighborhood children.*

Moira: *How would you know, you haven't been to see me in over ten years.*

Della: *We have to fix things first.*

Beth Ann: *I need to use the restroom.*

Della: *It's not working.*

Moira: *Better put that on your list.*

Della: *I thought you wanted to fix things up?*

Moira: *It may be beyond help.*

Trudi: *And filthy.*

Della: *It's been closed up for a long time.*

Moira: *No one cared about it.*

Della: *I cared.*

Moira: *No you haven't, not until now and dad's gone.*

Della: *I cared. I just didn't know what to do, or who actually owns the estate?*

The room got quite. Beth Ann asked timidly, "Has anyone seen the will yet?"

I held my breath, waiting for the big climax to this scene, but instead of an answer we got that unearthly crack of the front door; "Furnace man."

Peter took his cue and exited stage left. I waited for a few seconds. When they obviously weren't going to discuss this delicate family matter in front of a stranger, I followed Peter's prompt.

* * *

Even though the air was colder in the great room, the dining room had been far from a heartwarming family reunion. I decided to continue snooping through the house, or maybe I should say inspecting it for needed artistic touches.

I did want to *touch* a few more things and get a feel for this family's estate. I had thought that it was Della's, but I think the cousins and the wicked sister would disagree. I walked up the creaking staircase. It seemed sound of structure; only achy from years of disuse. I kept my hands securely in my pockets, away from the wooden handrail, while climbing the steps. I did not want to get entranced in a past vision and go toppling down the stairs. Even though this house was old, and hadn't been utilized for years, I could imagine that there were many memories, piled as thick as the dust, on the furnishings.

Tucking my fingers into my coat sleeve, I turned a door knob and was facing a lavish bedroom. The room was completely round, *I must be on the second floor of the turret*, I thought. I walked to the antique Queen Anne bed. Caught up in the exquisite settings of the room I inadvertently reached over and smoothed my hand over the polished wood of the foot board, holding onto the rounded poster.

A scene materialized with hazy shafts of sunlight streaking across the room. There was a man standing at the open window staring out toward the lake. His white shirt was pulled tight across his shoulders. I felt uneasy, clinging to the bed post. I reached up and wiped a tear from my cheek. Norville was the name in my mind or being spoken quietly on my lips. I looked away and down to my dress; it was powder blue with small white dots. I pulled at it as the breeze snugged the fabric between my legs. I could see shoes as the man was standing close. I looked into his face as he began kissing me. I pulled away....

The man was gone, and the powder blue dress had disappeared. The room was here, but the window was closed and there wasn't any warm breeze. I took a deep breath while moving away from the bed and back into the hall.

I could still hear muffled voices rising from the dining room, so I took the opportunity to inspect the other rooms. Facing the lake side of the house were five bedrooms with their doors open. I glanced into each one down the line. Quilted bedspreads in a patchwork of color, glass globed lamps, sheer white curtains and a few other antique-style pieces of furniture decorated each of them; except for the last one. It was a child's room filled with toys and two small beds. As I was about to enter the little menagerie I heard the heaving groans of the wooden stairs. It was Peter and the furnace man.

"The heat will be coursing through these old radiators within a few hours. Also, the water has been turned on out at the main-valve." Peter reported, as if he needed to give an account to someone. And I assumed that I appeared safer than the mob downstairs.

As the radiators were checked in each room, the workers' voices became muffled behind the heavy walls. I noticed that the downstairs fanfare had ceased. It was eerily quiet. *Maybe they all killed each other,* I thought. Looking down the flight of stairs, I noticed for the first time that the upstairs railing and the hand rail were made from interlocking tree trunks. Root systems were used to anchor each of the supporting beams to the floor. The uniquely engineered rail-work was varnished in a honey maple. As I followed the lines of the entwined trees all the way to the first floor, I saw Della standing there peering up at me. She ran her fingers through her auburn hair as if to rake her thoughts from her brain.

"How did the episode end?" I asked, "or did the words *to be continued...* flash across the screen."

She smiled and said, "Thank goodness the curtain closed before the stage was spattered with blood."

I went down and hugged her, "I never would have imagined that you had such an unruly bunch of relatives. You're so nice."

"Time has taken its toll on them," she said in her kindhearted fashion, "They weren't always so bitter, except maybe Moira." We laughed as she tucked her arm into mine and walked me to the big front windows. "I'm not sure what their motives are," Della said, looking out over a landscape of frosty pines leading to the snow covered beach, "but, I can guess that Beth Ann and Trudi see dollar signs. As for Moira, I think she just doesn't want me to have it."

"The will should clear all that up?"

"I hope so. It seems that there's some confusion about the estate. Beth Ann said that in her father's will there was no mention of it. They assumed that the property had been kept for the families to share until the last of the three brothers passed away, that being my dad. Now they want to know if dad changed the will, cut them out, or if they are part owners of *True North*."

"I think the key word you said was *assumed*. What does the will say?"

"I don't know, neither does Moira, we've never seen it. His lawyer must have it. I'll call him tomorrow."

The radiators clanked to life as the water in them began to heat. We turned as Peter said, "Well Miss Della, it looks as if we'll have heat today. Tomorrow we can work on getting the plumbing fixed."

"Peter, you're unbelievable. Would you like to get some supper?"

"Thank you, but I have to be getting home to feed the dogs. I'll meet you here in the morning." With that, he pulled hard on the front door, "And we'll fix this, too." His laugh was easy as he tipped a hand to his cap in a friendly farewell.

I suggested to Della that she return to the Inn, take a hot bath and I'd bring food over in about an hour. I added, "I have a couple things I'd like to tell you about."

◆◆ **5** ◆◆

City sidewalks, busy sidewalks, dressed in holiday style...

Leaving *True North,* I rounded the corner onto the main street of Ottawa. Fluffy white snowflakes fell on our Christmas town. Storefronts were decked in green pine boughs, flickering white lights, ribbons of silver and the traditional sprigs of holly dotted with crimson berries. I felt a pride rising inside of me. The Holly Fest committee, of which I was a part of, chose a decorating theme for the three blocks of shops that lined Belle Star Road. I remembered Bob McMahon, director of the Ottawa Chamber of Commerce, saying how wintertime business was slower than in the summer months when tourists picked Lake Superior for their vacation destinations. We need to spruce up the town, offer a northwoods Christmas atmosphere to entice local shoppers to stay close to home while attracting out-of-towners to visit this little hamlet to get away from the bustle of the city for specialty gifts during the holidays. Bob was longwinded, but he had the right ideas, and we appreciated him for that.

He had also explained that snowmobilers, skiers and brave winter campers are the mainstay of winter's tourist economy in Ottawa, and other northern towns. I've always wished I knew how to promote these attributes. It's like they're the best kept secret.

Parking outside of Cricket's delicious little business, *Superior Sweets,* Christmas tunes fell as softly as the snow to my ears. Another one of the committee's creative inspirations was for music to be broadcasted downtown during each holiday season.

Before stepping into her shop, the scents of chocolate, berries and baked goods made my stomach rumble. Cricket was facing the back wall and said, "Hi Lexi, it's about time you stopped to fill me in."

"How do you always know it's me?" I asked, having wondered this for years.

"It's the only time Tabitha comes out of hiding," she said as a big yellow tabby darted toward me and began rubbing her purring head against my leg.

"Here I thought all these years that you were psychic; instead it's your cat." We laughed and hugged.

"How did it go at Della's today?"

She handed me a cranberry muffin and three chocolate dipped cherries resembling tiny mice with slivered almonds for ears, a miniature candy kiss nose and the cherry's stem for a tail. With two cups of coffee and a tray of more sweets, she ushered the cat and me to a northern-style bistro table; a round, cedar picnic table.

I told her about the cousins and Moira. "Can't wait to meet them," she said, "and there's two more?"

I nodded while holding the mousy confection by its tail and popping it nose first into my mouth. "I love these." Tabitha pawed at the little red tail sticking out from my lips. "How was business today?'

"Good, a bunch of hunky snowmobilers came in. They sure look like big, burly men in those suits, yum," she said licking her fingertips. I wasn't sure if she meant the chocolate or the guys were tasty. She got up and brought over a bag held neatly shut by a Velcro strap.

"I made these up just for snowmobilers. They're filled with high energy bars, chocolate covered pretzels, filled hard candies in bright blue wrappers and a Superior Sweets business card. It's compact to carry, easy to access while they're on the trail and it's a very discreet way of handing out my phone number. Ingenious, isn't it."

"You're good. How many did you sell?"

"One to each of them, along with some Mich-moose suckers, Superior muffins and other chocolates that can freeze and still please." We laughed.

I invited her to join me for supper with Della at the Belle Star Lighthouse Inn.

"I'll pick you on my way back through town; I'm getting pasties."

I drove two blocks to the corner where the main street, Belle Star Road, met Red Earth Road which headed east toward the Porcupine Mountains State Park or west toward the Keweenaw Peninsula. I wondered why Trudi had been on Red Earth Road this morning. The Belle Star headed straight up to the highway and was clearly the most accessible and well traveled route into town. Most visitors took that way. The Red Earth was a winding, treacherous road even in summer. It was mostly used by the locals or sightseers. It didn't make sense, unless she got lost, which given her apparent nature was highly possible.

At the Log Cabin Pasty Shop, I picked up the northern specialty and headed back up the main street toward Lake Superior. The hot Cornish pasty-pies, filled with meat, potatoes and rutabagas, smelled comforting. They'd be a hearty, stick-to-the-ribs meal on this cold night. A sign in the Log Cabin showed the pronunciation of the local favorite. There was a curved line above the '*a*', so that it was pronounced like past, not paste – pasty. The sign also explained how miners would take the traditional food for lunch in the mines, warming them on their headlamps. In more recent times, hunters and loggers would warm their lunch on their truck engines. I preferred getting them hot and fresh from the shop.

Cricket and I arrived at the Lighthouse Inn just past five o'clock. The sun had set and the sky was paled pink against the snow-filled clouds. Looking up at the lighthouse with its stone façade absorbing bits of the evening color, it was statuesque. Towering above the low growing junipers and leaf-bare tag alders it seemed to rise from the earth. Remnants of wild rose hips added burnt red blotches to the barren brown twigs. If it wasn't for the crisp white of the snow, and the green of the pines, the shoreline would look very bleak.

"Come on," Cricket said, "Its cold out here; even for me. I'm freezing tonight."

Bette McMahon met us at the reception desk of the Inn. She tossed her strawberry braid, flecked with gray, over her shoulder as she lifted her head and smiled, "Are you here to see Della? She's in the *William Riley*."

"Thanks," I said, "and when that nephew of yours gets home could you tell him we're here."

"He's out shoveling," she replied looking out the side window to see if she could spot Foster's youthful frame for which she kept a keen lookout for. Foster had explained how his aunt kept tabs on him like a mother bear protecting her cub.

"He'll probably follow the scent of the pasties," she said while fixing the collar of her stylish, buckskin jacket, "Even through these stone walls he'll smell them. He can track down food better than Peter's bloodhounds. Probably eats more than all his dogs put together."

"I know," said Cricket, "he devoured a whole loaf of nut bread and two scones today at the shop. We better eat our share of supper before he finishes the walkways."

Della was posed by the window, framed in royal blue draperies, when we knocked and then let ourselves in. "This is where Joe and I spent our five year anniversary," she walked over and touched the framed coast guard photos hanging on the wall, "Lots of memories. Joe read me each of the stories about the *Coasties* stationed here. How they braved the storms to save countless lives and received awards for their heroism."

She moved over to a cherry wood dresser. Its top was encased in glass and held an odd array of objects. "Each of these little treasures was given to those courageous men and the lighthouse keepers as tokens of gratitude from families of the survivors." Her eyes looked back toward the window, "I wish they'd have been around to save Joe."

Then, looking back at us she said, "I just got off the phone with Jenny and I talked to Joey. He's going to see Santa tomorrow. There's a parade in Door County and a party for the kids afterward."

"Will they be coming up for Holly Fest?" I asked, "If you're still here?" I knew that was a big concern for Della. It was the holidays and she was away from her family, at least the good part of her family, her daughter and grandson.

Shaking away the nostalgia she turned, "Something smells good."

While we ate Della told us about Lighthouse Bill, the lightkeeper who supposedly haunts this room. "I've heard of him," Cricket said, "but never had the chance to get in this room."

"Can you feel anything?" I asked. She thought a minute, then realizing that I was teasing, said, "He's right there behind you. I think he wants your food."

* * *

A hand reached around and grabbed my pasty. I jumped, and maybe squealed a little, as a big mouth loomed over my food. "Give me your food," he said in a fake zombie voice. I smacked Foster's leg as he sat down next to me on the four-poster bed being used as a picnic spot.

"I've read about Lighthouse Bill," Foster said with food tucked in his cheek, "There was a big storm and the light went out. He went to relight the beacon, which was done by hand back then, and a bolt of lightening hit him."

"Did he get the lamp lit?" I asked.

"Yep, and received all kinds of medals for being killed in the line of duty. Too bad he wasn't around to accept them, but his niece did, and then donated then to the lighthouse."

"Who was his niece?" Cricket asked, ever snoopy.

"All I remember is that her surname was the good old Canadian name of Mackenzie."

"The name is familiar. Maybe, they came to our parties at *True North*," Della said.

We finished our food and Della went to the desk and lit the brass lantern, "For Lighthouse Bill; we honor him, and wish him rest; someplace else."

"To Bill," we chimed, and saluted his memory.

I seized the opportunity, "Speaking of memories, I was wondering if you remember a time at the estate when a little girl broke a tray of glasses?"

Della looked at me with her inquisitive one eyebrow raised, "Yes, I do. And how would you know about that?"

I fidgeted with the laces of my boots, feeling a little over warm and said, "Well, I went snooping today while you were having your family discussion." When I looked up, her hazel eyes were hard to read. The greens and browns were like camouflage in the woods hiding her thoughts and emotions.

She came and sat by me, took my hands in hers and said, "There are many memories inside of that old house. Some of them are good, others are not so fond."

"I know. I experienced a few of them today."

Cricket, who had obviously been holding her breath or possibly covering her mouth, couldn't contain herself any longer and said, "Lexi, did you see anything? What was it like? I would have died to have lived back in the forties and fifties, it was so romantic."

I looked at Della. It was her home and her memories, so it was up to her if I should tell these tales.

She looked at Cricket, "It was wonderful. Each summer held a new adventure at the lodge. We'd pack the car and head north. My parents loved it up here and their moods would change the closer we got to Ottawa. My dad would begin to whistle old movie tunes and mom would sing along. They'd talk about party plans and their friends. It was magical."

"What about the parties?" Cricket asked, "Were they as grand as the movies make them out to be with dancing and sweet innocent love affairs?"

Della laughed, "Actually they were. The house was filled with people laughing and music on the record player. There were always other children to play with. We'd dance on the beach and explore the woods. Sometimes the cousins would be there, but we often planned our vacations at separate times, so that the business always had one of the brothers manning the ship yards. We really didn't see each other that often as kids, or as we got older. We varied in age so that even in school we were in different grades. Our mothers tolerated each other, but were not actually friends. Of course, we'd spend holidays together, mostly because that's what the men wanted."

She gazed out toward the lake beyond the lighthouse, "Now I'm rambling with old family stuff that you probably don't find at all interesting." She stood and walked to the window.

"Actually, it's very interesting," I said, and Foster and Cricket both agreed.

"What happened today?" Foster asked, "I saw the sheriff take that car crash lady out to the Northern Lights Motel earlier, but then I spent the day at the newspaper. So I think I missed a bunch of action."

Della and I told him about the family coming to the estate while Peter was working on getting the place up and functional. Della took a deep breath and asked for the rest of my adventuring through the lodge. I explained about being on the cedar chest and seeing the glasses break.

And then, I told her about the scene in the bedroom with the man and woman. "Did your mom have a powder blue dress?" I asked.

"I don't remember one," she said, tilting her head and eyes to the right accessing her memory, "She wore bright sunny floral dresses or cotton shirts, to compliment her brunette hair. Pastels, especially blue were not her colors, or mine." She brushed at her scarlet cardigan and asked, "What did the man look like?"

I closed my eyes to remember the scene and said, "It was kind of hazy, and the light from the window made him appear silhouetted and muted, but he was probably about six foot tall with broad shoulders in a white cotton shirt pulled too tightly across his back. He had a strong build; heavy but not fat. When he was closer, I saw that he was good looking with dark hair and a mustache," I opened my eyes and said, "It was so fleeting, only a few minutes of time had passed. Whatever had happened at that moment must have created some strong emotions for them to have lasted all these years."

"He sounds dreamy," Cricket said.

Foster added, "And, he fits the description of nearly every other man from that era."

Della shook her head and said, "Except, that room was only used by my dad and his brothers. Want to take a look at some pictures?"

We bundled up and drove over to the estate for another nighttime rendezvous with the ghosts at *True North*.

◆◆ **6** ◆◆

It came upon a midnight clear, that glorious song of old...

Crack. *"Hi honey, were home,"* I said as the door once again bellowed our arrival into the lodge.

"It's warmer in here tonight, but it's dark. Where are the lights, Della?"

"I'm not sure." We fumbled around; sliding our hands against the walls looking for a switch.

"Didn't you bring a flashlight?" Foster asked me.

"Oh yeah, I forgot." I pulled my mini Mag-light from my pocket and proceeded to shine it around the room. "Here it is," I said, flicking up a single switch.

"Wow!" said Cricket. Above us hung an enormous, stained glass chandelier trimmed in brass. It lit the pinewood lined foyer and staircase with a golden glow, accentuating the details of the tree-formed railings. "This is amazing," she continued, "what are the other rooms like?"

We moved through the lodge flicking on lights while Cricket oowed and aawed through the entire mansion. "This has to be worth a fortune," she said.

"I imagine the cousins think so too," Della replied, "that's probably why they've finally shown some interest in it, and my sister too."

Coming down from the second floor, I stopped sharply. Cricket bumped me from behind, "What is it?"

"Listen," I said in a whisper, "I hear something in the kitchen."

"Maybe it's a mouse stirring," she said, breathing so close to my ear that I had to nudge her back.

Foster came down to where I was standing, grabbed my hand and led us through the foyer, into the great room, around the corner to the dining room where we stood staring at the noises coming from behind the kitchen door. One step at a time we approached the painted wood door. There was a clatter of a pan, then a shuffle and a hiss and a bang.

Foster reached forward and inched the door open just as a chair toppled over with a crash mixed with a screech. We pushed in. There, lying on the floor was a woman, sprawled among splintered wood and broken glass. She wrestled her black leather boots from under the broken chair, straightened her red cashmere sweater, looked up and said, "Hello Della, I was putting on tea."

"Blair," Della said with surprise and then asked, "What were you doing?"

"Like I said, I was putting on tea."

"But, there's no water."

"Sure there is. After the air finished spattering out of the lines there was plenty of water."

Della was puzzled. When we'd left earlier today the plumbing hadn't been completed.

"There was a very nice man here earlier, Peter Hollywood, or something like that, and he got water for us."

"*Us?*" Della asked.

"Hazel and I."

"How did you get in?"

"That Mr. Hollingsworth was here. But, that didn't matter, the key is still in the log where it's always been," she said bending down to pick up the broken glass. "The chair must have given way while I was getting cups. I was just leaving when I heard you come in. So, I thought I'd make tea."

Della just stared at her cousin. She was in her late forties, very stylish from her professionally highlighted brunette hair to her tailored Merino wool slacks. She was thickening around her edges, but otherwise looked fit. Foster went over and began helping with the clean up. Cricket and I stood one on each side of our friend. It was either for protection or in case we had to hold Della back from committing a heinous act. Or possibly, we thought, she might faint. Her body language was changing with each word the women, Blair, spoke.

The tea kettle whistled. Della jumped. Blair righted herself, threw glass into the trash and said, "Tea's on."

Della said that she'd be right back, leaving us self-consciously standing in the kitchen with Blair, the other cousin who had now shown up in Ottawa with her sister Hazel. I conversationally inquired of the absent relative's whereabouts.

"Oh, she's back at the motel. A nice little place called the Windigo. Quite comfortable," she said. Turning toward Foster she asked, "Could you be dear and reach some more cups?"

I thought it was interesting how she described the Windigo as a nice little place. It was the town's most elaborate motel with high end rooms, a pool, hot tub and sauna. Three floors of luxury suites were designed after the lakeside lodging facilities of Mackinac Island. They came complete with balconies, handsome furnishings and a full continental breakfast each morning.

Della rejoined us in the great room where we sat on coarse-velvet, overstuffed furniture around a large round coffee table. She had brought with her a stack of photo albums. "I was bringing my friends over to show them some family photos," she said taking a seat next to me on the sofa. Cricket snuggled in on my other side and Foster took up a spot on the floor at my feet.

Blair, sitting alone, quite some distance away, said, "That sounds like fun, but I must go and check on Hazel." She took her cup to the kitchen, ran water and left through the side entrance with a, "See you tomorrow."

"The gang's all here," Della sighed, opening the first album. She began to narrate through the photos. After about a dozen pages of whose-who and how they fit into the family scheme, I spotted the man in the white cotton shirt. "There he is," I pointed.

"That's Uncle Norville, Blair and Hazel's dad."

"Norville, of course, the woman had whispered his name. I had forgotten."

Foster looked at me, a little confused, and said, "You heard her say his name?"

"Whisper it, or think it. Sometimes my visions aren't real clear, I've told you that. They feel fragmented, like I'm in someone else's body. It's hard to explain, but when I'm experiencing what someone else has seen, or what they've felt, I don't have all of their memory references to help out in deciphering what the information means. It's like seeing two minutes of a movie. And in most cases, unless there's a mirror directly ahead, I don't even know whose eyes I'm seeing through."

Foster nodded and put a hand on my knee, and said, "So, the guy was Norville True. Who was the woman?"

"Probably his wife, Aunt Patsy," Della said paging through the album, "Here's her picture."

She looked a lot like Blair with ash-brown hair and wide eyes, except she was heavy - very heavy. All eyes were on me. "I had the feeling this woman was slender. Was she ever thinner?"

"No, she was always a big woman," Della answered. We leafed through each of the remaining books. Della continued her family story about how the men had made their fortune building ships, the different homes they had lived in and summers in Ottawa. Cricket loved the party photos. She kept commenting on how she wished more of them were in color so we could see the beautiful dresses, and possibly spot the blue dress with white polka dots.

Foster offered to do some on-line research tomorrow, "The internet is a storehouse of public knowledge. I'll run a few checks on your cousins."

As we retraced our steps through the lodge turning off lights I noticed an odd sound coming from the den. On cue, Cricket said, "I smell trouble." The clatter began again as it had the night before.

Della, wide eyed and expectant, headed for her father's den. As she approached the door, the noise stopped. We were on her heels and nearly pushed her through the opening. A book was lying on the floor by the desk. Foster picked it up and read the cover - *Superior Hauntings*. He handed it to Della. She held it in front of her with both hands. Rubbing her thumbs on the cover, her eyes bore through it as if looking back into the past. She said, "Evenings, when it was too chilly to sit on the beach, Moira and I would sit by the fire while dad read to us. This was my favorite book with its tales of ship captains, monsters from the deep waters and lost treasures. The last story I remember him reading was of Belle Star."

She paged through the book remembering the tale, "Belle's father was a ship captain. He was bringing her fiancé and all his daughter's belongings to her over the rough September waters of Lake Superior when a terrible storm rose. The beacon went out in the lighthouse. Belle braved the elements, relit the light and stayed on the catwalk all night watching for the ship. My dad had never finished that story. We had to leave the lodge because mother became ill. When we returned, we were teenagers and didn't sit by the fireside anymore. He had marked the place where we were to continue reading with a sheet of his stationary folded into a neat rectangle."

She paged through the book with fervor. "It's not here. It was always here. I remember one time opening the book and it stuck tight into the binding. He'd wedge it in to mark our last page." She was becoming hysterical as she shook the book furiously.

"It's okay, we'll find it," I said while looking on the floor by the desk. Foster was checking under chairs. Cricket was inspecting the fireplace. There was no sign of a book marker.

Della moved over to the far wall that was completely lined with books arranged neatly on its shelves. "It had been right here," she said, pointing to a gap in the bindings. "How did it get over by the desk?" Foster spoke the question we were all thinking.

"Maybe the ghost did it," Cricket said.

"Or my cousin."

◆◆ 7 ◆◆

Walking in a winter wonderland...

Morning sunlight glistened off the snow. Clouds passed with the night. My boots crunched in time with the holiday carols greeting everyone in downtown Ottawa. Jedadiah Buckland, better known as Whistler, sat on the park bench in front of the Loose Moose gift shop. Every Friday morning he waited for his granddaughter, Macy, to finish work at the Voyageur Gas Station. It was their shopping day. He could meet her at the filling station and walk across the street to the supermarket, the Captain's Co-op, but he preferred giving his business to his old friend, Bart, owner of the Ottawa General Store.

"Good morning Whistler," I said from across the street, "Are you coming to Holly Fest?"

"Wouldn't miss it," he said and gestured for me come across the street by him.

"Do you think you could help me find a present for my granddaughter? It's hard for an old codger like me to know what to get a twenty-year-old girl. I could pick her out some books or a scarf but, I thought that you might have a better idea."

"She was mentioning that she needed a flash-drive for her computer, so that she could download information from the library to do her on-line schoolwork at home. It probably costs around thirty dollars."

He rubbed his face and said, "That sounds perfect. I'll be selling some furs later today. Thorny and I got a few fox and a couple of mink last week; nice and prime they were. So, that should cover it and maybe get her a scarf, too, hey?"

"I'll get it for you in Houghton before Christmas."

I said goodbye and a few seconds later heard Macy asking him if he was giving me trouble. He told her to never mind. I waved back at her. They went to Bart's and I went into the Shipwreck where Della, Cricket and Foster were huddled at a bigger back table.

"Scheming before breakfast?" I asked.

"Never on an empty stomach," Cricket replied while rubbing her bulging, wool sweater. "Actually, Della called her lawyer this morning, and guess what?"

"What?" I asked.

"The will is missing," Della said, "and other documents in the file."

"What do you mean *missing*?" I asked.

"He said that they were in a fireproof filing cabinet in his office where he keeps all his important documents. When I called, he went to check on them and they were gone. He asked his secretary and she hadn't taken them, and no one else had access to the cabinet."

"Well, obviously someone did," I said, "or maybe he put them somewhere else."

"I questioned him about that and he assured me they would not be anywhere else. He's checking into it and will call me later. I did ask him when he had last seen the paperwork. He said that my father had been in there about a year ago to make sure everything was in order. That was right before he went to the nursing home. I remember driving him there. He also said that my father should have a copy of the will, but I've never seen it."

"Can I get you some coffee?" Allisa asked as she eyed Foster. When he didn't return the gesture she continued, "Our special today is the Sailor Boy, buckwheat pancakes and ham served with Aunt Mabel's special Christmas spiced apples."

The door jingled in Sheriff Golden and Peter Holloway, not Hollywood or Hollingsworth. They sat down with us. We all ordered the daily special, except for Judd. "I know," said Allisa, "Aunt Mabel told me you always order the same thing, the Captain's Special." She smiled proudly at herself. Sauntering away from the table, with her hips swaying in sync with the coffee in the pot, she was probably hoping Foster was watching. He hadn't even glanced at her as he folded his arms over the canoe imprinted on his Boundary Waters sweatshirt. It was one of the many shirts he always wore, advertising some not-so-far off paradise in our great, northern world.

"I see you fixed the plumbing last night at the lodge," Della said to Peter, "and met my cousin Blair."

"Yes, I did, on both counts," he smiled at her, "She snuck in on me. Caught me by surprise and I banged my head under the sink. No damage, to my head anyway, I think I may have chipped the cast iron basin."

We laughed. Peter was as tough as they come, a real honest to goodness man. Even when talking about others, which he rarely did, he tried to see the upside of people.

"Is she the last of them?" he asked.

"I don't believe any of you have met Hazel yet," she said heaving a deep sigh while setting down her coffee cup, "Hazel is different, and for lack of a better term, *crazy*."

"Crazy, like in wild?" Foster asked.

"Or crazy like in loony?" said Cricket.

"Like in loony," Della said quietly, "she was born that way. She's not slow or challenged. I think that's the correct way of saying it. She's just plain crazy. Never actually been diagnosed, or treated for that matter, she just does strange things. She's not mean or destructive, just crazy."

At that very moment the bell jingled in Blair, and Hazel. We pushed a few more tables together as Hazel skittered across the room. She was in her late thirties, blonde, pretty and within a couple seconds I could see, yes she was crazy. She came up to Della, smelled her hair, flipped it a few times, smelled it again and then let out a high pitched, but soft squeal and said, "It's Della, Blair, it's Della!"

She straightened Della's collar then wrapped her arms around her in a big bear hug. Hazel then let go of Della, sat down at the table and said, "Hi I'm Hazel." She picked up a menu and said, "I love blueberries." She was quiet for a moment, set the menu down and said, "Christmas is in a week and I have lots of shopping to do," and then looking right at the sheriff said, "Did you know my Uncle Carsen died, I liked him." She looked for the waitress and then back at the menu. She was exhaustingly hard to follow, but actually quite nice, like Della had said.

Blair sat next to Hazel and ordered for her. Hazel ate in complete silence. Blair asked about each of us, not retaining any of it I'm sure, but it made for good breakfast talk.

As we were getting up to leave, Hazel said, "I'm going to live in the big house on Lake Superior."

We all stared at her, shifting our attention quickly to Blair. "Oh, don't listen to her, she rambles."

"Why did you come here, Blair?" Della asked.

"Because…Hazel wanted to."

"What do you mean Hazel wanted to, Hazel probably doesn't even remember Ottawa."

"Oh, but she does. She talks about it all the time. She likes the beach. And she remembers playing in the big house with all the toys, just like you and I do," Blair said to Della, and then leaning a little closer thinking no one else could hear, "Remember cousin, she's crazy not dumb."

Della backed away from her.

"I'm taking Hazel over to the house," she said. Looking at Peter, she continued "If I remember correctly Mr. Holiday will be going there also, to do some fixing up. Are you joining us Della?"

Grabbing up her cape, Della gestured her to lead the way.

Before we left, Judd grabbed my arm and pulled me back from the others, and said, "I ran a background check on that sports car and its owner yesterday. Her name is Trudi B. True and she lives in a little town in Wisconsin. She's had a bunch of speeding tickets and few drunk-driving charges that seem to have disappeared off of her record. I talked to the sheriff down there, we worked together about ten years ago, and he said that she's trouble. She acts like a big shot with lots of daddy's money that she waves around, but she actually lives in a run-down apartment building and works at a local tavern. And, it just happens to be the same watering hole frequented by the town judge. That could explain the vanishing drunk-driving charges."

"Thanks, I'll tell Della."

Cricket, Foster and I hopped into Della's Navigator for a quick chat. I told her what Judd had said about Trudi. Foster said he'd browse the Internet today and see what he could dig up.

Cricket said that her sister, Jana, knew the Beck girls from school: Faith, Hope and Charity. They would love to snoop around at the Windigo, their parent's motel. "Oh don't worry" she continued, "I won't tell her anything. I'll make up some kind of fun girl story."

I was meeting with Lyda Waverly, owner of the Northern Lights Motel and Restaurant, to work on Holly Fest decorations. I could check out Beth Ann and Trudi. "Where is Moira staying?" I asked. No one knew. Della said she'd find out. We made arrangements to meet back here at lunch time.

* * *

Lyda was going over paperwork with her cook when I arrived at the Northern Lights.

"Hi Lexi," she said, "I'll be right with you. We're almost finished with the menu for Holly Fest, and all the Christmas parties we have booked this year. Vivian's going to be busy."

"So will you missy," the robust sixty year old cook said as she snatched her apron from the counter, "You go ahead, I can finish this. I think everything is here, I just need to place an order and we'll be ready to whip up a feast fit for Santa himself."

"She loves to cook," Lyda said watching Vivian leave the office, "I'd be dead in the water without her."

"I think she knows it," I said, "You have a beautiful restaurant."

"Actually, its dad's, I just run it," she said, "and I need to check on him before we start if you don't mind."

"I'd love to see him," I said and followed her through the back door to their private quarters.

Elwood Waverly was seated in a big rocker recliner. He was wearing tan slacks and a hunter green chamois shirt. Even at seventy-eight he was a good looking man. "Dad, do you remember Lexi Marx?"

He tried to stand, which took all his effort, so I quickly sat next to him on the adjacent chair, "Good morning Mr. Waverly, how are you today."

"Good young lady, and how about yourself?"

We talked about the snow and Christmas, he was as sharp as a good fish hook, maybe sharper. Whistler had told me how Elwood Waverly had caught the prettiest girl in town, Lyda's mother, Meredith. She was a real catch, Whistler had said, all the boys tried to net that one, but Elwood used the right bait. According to Whistler, he wrote her poetry and brought flowers. Then he reeled her in with a marriage proposal on a moonlit night on the beach. Whistler also said that Elwood was one of the richest boys in town, but that wasn't as romantic as all the other things Elwood did. He wanted to believe Meredith chose Elwood because of the romance, not the money.

"I hear that some of the True girls are in town," Mr. Waverly said.

"All of them, I think; a total of six."

"I also heard that Carsen passed away. He was good man, unlike his brothers."

That was interesting I thought, and even though I wanted to interrogate him right here and now I politely asked, "You knew the True family?"

He nodded, "They had big parties over at their place. We all went with our families to share in the fun, and the wealth. Carsen was always a good host. We'd bring beer and casseroles to share. Him and his wife would put them out and be gracious. The brothers weren't so obliging. They would stick our food in the kitchen for the help to eat, and flaunt their expensive tastes at us. We all felt that way, the whole town. Hugh was a worthless drunk that Caroline endured, probably because of his cash. Norville was the worst. His high minded wife would make fun of the women and children; mostly how they talked and dressed. It was dreadful. They were dreadful. But, they had money, so everyone put on nice faces and let them act however they wanted."

Lyda returned with breakfast for her dad, "Sorry it took so long, I had to speak with Vivian about a disturbance in the dining room this morning. Seems a couple of our guests complained about the food."

"Let me guess," I said, "Beth Ann and Trudi B. True."

Elwood huffed. Lyda gave him a silencing look, and said to me, "You're right."

"Not surprising," Elwood Waverly said to his plate of food.

"Dad, Vivian said if you'd like more to eat to give her ring."

Before we left, I looked around the room. There were photos of blonde, blue-eyed Lyda at every age from birth until her now forty years of age. I did the math. Her father would have been thirty-eight when she was born. I wonder if her mother was a lot younger than him.

Lyda looked exhausted as she said, "I shouldn't say anything, but Vivian is ready to kick those women out. I had to calm her down. We need to be renting rooms, that's our business."

As we entered a room off of the lobby she said, "I only have about an hour to work on the decorations. There's so much to be done around here, especially now that dad can't walk very well. He did so much. Maybe it's his time to take a break."

As we made huge silver snowflakes out of glittered papers I gave her a shortened version of the True sisters' arrival in Ottawa.

"I've always liked Della, even as kids we'd play together during the summer. Blair, Beth and Moira were older and Trudi and Hazel younger, so I didn't really get to know them. And besides, Della was the nicest. When I was young, I use to wish she was my sister. After mom left I knew I'd be an only child," she said.

We finished most of our project for the day. I offered to take the rest home, as I had more time at the moment. She thanked me and promised to keep tabs on the two True sisters. As I was leaving, I spotted Beth Ann and Trudi getting into an older Jeep Cherokee. I decided to follow, as discreetly as I could, in the banana-mobile.

They headed toward the drive to *True North* but, instead turned before it into the parking lot of Pirate's Cove Saloon and Coffee House. I pulled up to the Fern and Forest Floral and waited until they were inside before heading back to town. At the Shipwreck Café I took a booth seat while waiting for my lunch companions. Allisa had given me a cup of strong coffee. As I drank it, I looked at the stately black and white photograph hanging on the wall. I'd seen it many times. This time I read the story printed below it:

The Mesquite, a steel coast guard cutter, was filling in for her sister ship, the Sundew, attempting to collect navigational markers on December 4, 1989. It drifted too close to a reef and the rough December weather did the rest, firmly lodging the Mesquite on a rock ledge. The weather quickly worsened and the waves began to pound her against the shoal. A state of general confusion aboard the ship prevented an effective plan of action. After a few hours the hull was badly damaged and the ship's cabins were taking on water. A distress call was put out and the crew was removed by a passing freighter. Fierce storms battered the cutter and crusted her with a thick layer of ice. She spent the winter on the reef due to unremitting weather and was not salvageable. The Mesquite was the first Coast Guard vessel to be declared as a casualty.

Reading the ship's account, I realized how unforgiving Lake Superior's storms can be. I wondered if Della's family was a winter storm about to unleash itself, pounding unremittingly until all became unsalvageable. I feared that a vicious squall was gathering.

♦♦   **8**   ♦♦

Do you hear what I hear?...

"The will has been stolen," Della said after settling herself in beside me in the booth. Cricket and Foster sat across from us.

"What do you mean stolen?" Cricket blurted out.

"Not so loud, I haven't told anyone yet," Della said looking around as if spies, or worse gossips, were lurking in the café. "After inspecting his file cabinet, the lawyer said it was jimmied."

"Who could do that?" I questioned, "Do any of your cousins have that type of skill."

Foster said, "Trudi seems like the sort who'd have friends in low places. Or, the others could have hired someone."

"I don't know," said Della, "It's crazy."

"Hazel?" Cricket said.

"I doubt she has the brain power for it," Della said, "She'd probably forget what she was doing and start making little figures from the paper clips."

I relayed my conversation with Elwood Waverly about the brothers. Della was relieved that her father had been pegged the *good one*. I also mentioned the sisters' visit to the Pirate's Cove.

"Kat's a smart lady," I said, "She would have spotted them as trouble even through a blizzard. Maybe we can pay her a visit tonight for a cup of cheer and see what they talked about."

Foster had found out that Beth Ann and Trudi were selling everything they owned on e-bay.

"They must have a cash flow problem," Della surmised, "What about Blair, anything on her?"

"She owns an investment business with a website," Foster explained, "It seems to be on the up and up. She probably runs it from her home."

"So, she can care for Hazel," Della again presumed, "She's driving a BMW, she must be doing good."

"Moira," Foster said, "Is no where to be found.

"That's not surprising," Della nodded, "She likes to live under the radar, or off they grid as you'd say."

"So why would any one of them steal the will?" Cricket whispered.

Della shrugged. Foster said, "Pick any one of many reasons; greed being on the top. That property has to be worth a fortune. So, Beth Ann and Trudi would be the most likely candidates."

"Wouldn't they get a third of the value?" Cricket asked. Della nodded slightly.

I answered, "That's how estates are usually divided."

"But," Foster added, "It's only property, not cash, if it's not sold. And property actually requires money for upkeep and taxes. They haven't been chiming in about the renovation, have they?"

Della shook her head, no.

"How would stealing the will help them?" I asked.

Foster began to explain the complexities of a property going into probate court. As he finished I looked at Della, and asked, "What's wrong?"

"What if it's Moira causing trouble," she paused, "and what if they think it's me?"

"Why would they do that?" I asked.

"Oh let's see, maybe because I was always the favorite, the outgoing one. Even at the ship yard all the workers would chime *Della B. True to me.*" she paused, "One summer, when I was about eight, my dad, who was into his drink, put me up on his shoulder and waved his arm out and said *Della B. True, one day this is all going to be yours.*" She sighed, "He meant well, but from that day on Moira was even meaner, the cousins even more spiteful. He cursed me with those words."

"Now Della that's not true," Cricket said, and laughed despite herself at her little pun. Della laughed too, "I know. It was just dreadful having all of them at the house. It was a circus. Then to top it off, I feel like a terrible person for wishing they'd just go away. It is Christmas, and I should be more hospitable."

I jumped in, "You are the most gracious person I know. Some people are just more difficult to be nice to."

"How about we throw them a party?" Cricket said.

"Or invite them to Holly Fest, show them the town spirit?" I offered.

"Or take them for a long walk onto the lake?" Foster said, "Just kidding."

That afternoon I accompanied Della to *True North* where she'd disclose the information about the missing will to her relatives. She gathered all of them around the dining table and dropped the news like a big ice ball. There wasn't any warning. She stood tall, brushed a long silvering strand of hair away from her shoulder and said it.

The cacophony began. Accusations were thicker and sharper than the icebergs on the lake. Della stood there. She did not participate very much. I think her father would have been proud of his daughter. Peter stepped in to ask a question and seeing the futility of it retreated to his work. I stayed and listened.

Later, at the Pirate's Cove we found a table and while waiting for Cricket and Foster talked with Kat Wikerson. "The older of the two ordered coffee, but the younger had an *Appletini*."

Always the good proprietor, she started with their drink orders, and then continued, "We passed the normal chit chat back forth; who they were, where they lived, that kind of thing. I got busy with other customers so, they started talking amongst themselves." She stopped for a second and patted her ears, "But, I've got bartender ears; you can block out an obnoxious customer or hone in on a good piece of gossip.

"So I tuned in, mostly because I heard them talking about you, Lexi, and Della. Even though we've never met before," she said to Della, "any friend of Lexi's is someone I'd like to know. Anyway, they were talking about the big estate, and their families. They said they couldn't understand why you'd be wasting money fixing up that old place. It was outdated and worthless, as it was. They seemed more interested in the property, *prime piece of real estate* they said. Then they mentioned a buyer. That was all I heard, someone turned on the jukebox and anytime I got close they'd shut up."

"Thanks Kat, that was a lot," I said, "Let me know when you want to see a movie, or something, my treat."

"Sounds fun; if I can ever get away from here. Maybe my brother would take a night shift after Christmas when it slows down." She went to get our drinks. I watched as she tossed a bar towel over her shoulder, slid behind the bar and began mixing. It was all very natural to her. I could tell she'd been doing this for years. Not in Ottawa, she'd only moved here a year ago, but running a coffee shop/tavern seemed to be as comfortable as an old quilt to Kat.

Cricket and Foster snowballed into the saloon covered from top-knot to boot-bottom in thick wet flakes. As they disrobed, melting splatters followed them to our table. "When did it start snowing again?" I asked leaning away from the icy shower they were unintentionally offering.

"About a half hour ago, and it's coming down hard," Foster said giving his hair a shake.

Before I could tell them about Kat's conversation with the cousins, Blair heaved herself through the door, pushed snowflakes off her eyelashes and scanned the room. "Della," she nearly ran toward her, "Hazel is gone."

* * *

"What do you mean she's gone? Sit down."
"I don't want to sit down. Hazel is missing. I left her at the motel and when I got back she was gone." Blair was pacing, and then she grabbed Della, "We have to find her. It's awful outside."
"Blair, calm down. Maybe she went to the gas station." Della tried to sooth her.
"I already checked there; and the grocery store, and every last place I could think of."
"Okay, we'll call the sheriff, now sit and we'll get some coffee," She asked Foster to call Judd, and Cricket to get coffee, and whispered to her, "See if there's any valium flavored creamer."
As Blair sipped the coffee Della continued with soothing scenarios, maybe she was using the restroom when you stopped at the restaurant, or you may have been in one place while she moved on to another. It was working mildly.
"The sheriff will be right here," Foster said.
Cricket added, "I called the Becks in case she shows up back at the motel. I gave them Della's cell number."
Sheriff Judd Golden came through the door in a matter of minutes. He took all the information and told Blair, "We have a community phone network here in Ottawa. You just sit quietly and I'll get it rolling." He went to the phone and made one call. I knew that this would start a chain reaction coursing through the businesses and homes of Ottawa. Each person had another person to call who in turn called another, it only took about twenty minutes for everyone to be contacted and a return call made to the sheriff.
While we waited, Della called Beth Ann and Trudi.

"Does anyone know where Moira is staying?" Della asked. Foster piped in, "She's staying with Thorndike Hendershot."

"Thorny?" Cricket said. Foster just shrugged.

Della said, "He took a shine to her when we were kids. Lexi can you call her, please."

"Anyplace else I'd say that was weird," Foster said, "but in Ottawa it's just some old guy being nice to a kid."

"He wasn't so old back then, and Moira wasn't a kid," Blair added, "She was sixteen."

"Okay, that's on the verge of being wrong," Foster amended his previous assumption.

Another blast of snow swept through the tavern as Beth Ann and Trudi came in. The older cousin tromped snow all the way to Blair, and gave her a pat-pat-hug. Trudi was actually quiet.

Sheriff Golden's phone rang. No one had seen Hazel. It was now official, she was missing.

"My deputy has the volunteer fire department on their way to the community center, I'll be meeting them," Judd said to all of us. "Foster you and the ladies meet Peter at the motel. He'll want to start from there. I've already called him and he's loading the dogs. It's bad out. Be careful."

I handed the phone to Della, "Moira says she's all tucked in for the night."

Della snatched the phone and moved away from her cousins, so they couldn't hear. I heard. I think her exact words were, *Now you listen here Moira B. True, you get your skinny little ass down here right now or I'll come out there and get you and drag you in your 'jammies right down main street... do you understand?*

"Moira will meet us at the motel," Della said as we bundled up for the unexpected storm's onslaught. We drove all the vehicles over to the Windigo. Foster drove Blair, which he volunteered to do. She had a Beamer, and he was thrilled.

Peter was pulling around the corner onto Belle Star just ahead of us. He had the dog box on the truck rather than the tool box. Poking out of holes cut into the sides of the wood were three heads. Two were unmistakably his bloodhounds, Gumshoe and Ruby. The other one's gray nose and ears were covered in snow. This made Ghost appear even more ethereal.

The Becks' and their three children were waiting for us in the lobby. As we entered, the middle daughter, Hope, was tugging on her mother's arm saying *Momma I saw....* Momma wouldn't listen, but I could hear her. The mother scooted her back and came over to speak with Peter, who was talking to Blair.

"You aren't going to bring those dogs in here, are you Mr. Holloway?" she asked.

"No m'am that won't be necessary," he politely said, "Miss True and I are going to go up to her room and get one of her sister's shirts. That's all the dogs will need." Then he turned to Della and said, "Would you come too, please." As Della stepped forward Trudi began to object, and Blair argued while Della defended herself. Peter whistled a single high-pitched note which stung my ears.

"Ladies, the more time you waste fighting, the harder it will to track in this snow," he said ushering the two women away from the group. Blair took the lead to the second floor room she and Hazel were sharing. Just before they reached the door Della turned and called to me, "Come here please dear." I was so glad she was thinking, because I couldn't figure out how I was going to get into that room.

As I came to Della's side, Blair was handing Peter a light blue denim shirt, "She had this on earlier today," she said.

"This will work just fine," Peter nodded. Straightened a dog leash he had strapped across his chest, he headed back down the hallway.

"I'm feeling kind of fuzzy and faint," Della said, "maybe it was that drink. I need to sit a minute."

"I can stay with her, you go ahead and catch up with Peter," I said to Blair.

She thanked me and hurried off.

"That was too easy," Della said, "now you do your thing. I'll watch the door."

I looked at the dresser. By the television, there was a hairbrush with ash blonde hair in it. *This must be Hazel's* I thought and picked it up.

The room grew lighter. I was staring into the mirror, humming a Christmas tune, and brushing my hair while thinking how pretty I looked. I heard Blair say she was leaving. I just kept humming... Dashing through the snow, in a one horse open sleigh... I stopped brushing and could see a woman's face looking though the window. I could see it in the mirror. I turned around and it was gone. There was snow falling, little white flakes of snow. I began dancing.

That was it. "She must have dropped the brush," I said my thoughts out loud. After recapping to Della what I'd seen, I apologized, "It's not much help."

" Do you know whose face it was in the window?"

I shook my head, "I think I've seen her. She was old, but I can't put a name to her."

As we returned to the lobby, Moira pulled up in a big black Hummer. "Sweet," Foster's eyes sparkled like the chrome he was gazing at, "I'll drive that."

"Not in this lifetime little boy," Moira replied flicking her scarf at him and asking Della, "So what's the plan?"

Cricket stepped forward and said, "The sheriff called and said that we should split up and drive the town roads checking anywhere and everywhere. The search and rescue teams are canvassing the woods adjacent to town and Peter has his dogs out looking for a scent trail."

While they were sorting out the driving arrangements, I took Cricket and went to find little Hope Beck. "She saw something," I told her, "and her mom shuffled her way."

"Yeah, why listen to a kid," Cricket said, "What do they know? Jana said they spend a lot of time in the pool. Let's check there first."

Jana was right. There they were, all three of the little stairstep Beck girls. "Hey kids," Cricket said, "did you she that lady that everyone is looking for?"

Hope said, "The crazy lady? Yeah, I saw her when I got home from school. She was talking to an old lady out in the parking lot."

"Did you know the old lady and did she leave with her?" I asked.

"No, I didn't know her, and when I headed to the kitchen for a snack they were still outside talking."

"Thanks."

As we left the pool room I said to Cricket, "That's the best lead yet. We better tell the sheriff."

By the time we returned to the lobby Trudi and Beth Ann had began their search with Foster driving their Cherokee. He would be better at navigating the streets. Moira had Blair by her jacket and was boosting her into the Hummer. Della was waiting for us. We told her about the Beck girl seeing Hazel with an old woman. I told Cricket about seeing an old woman in the window, or Hazel seeing her actually.

"So, who's the old woman?" Cricket asked to no one in particular. We were stumped, so went to assist in the search.

We could see Peter's truck moving slowly along the Red Earth Road. We watched for a few minutes as he backed up, and then moved forward again. I called him on my cell phone, "Do you want help."

"Sure, come on up here. I could use your lights."

As we pulled up behind him, he was opening one of the dog doors and hoisted out Ghost. The dog was sleek, gray and all legs. He was a beautiful purebred Weimaraner. Peter held the denim shirt for the dog to smell and then sent him off into the woods. As Peter came over to Della's window, he said, "The dogs keep scenting something. I'm going to let Ghost work it for a bit. I can't imagine that girl wandering back into there." We told him about Hazel speaking with an old woman, but he didn't have any ideas on who she was either.

Ghost came back to the road and then retraced the trail back in again. He'd bark a few times before going silent. The night was so still. Snow falling is very quiet. There wasn't any wind, which was unusual. So, when Ghost began bawling, loud and long, it rang through the night.

"That's my cue," said Peter, "I'm heading in." He handed me a radio and said, "Stay with the dogs, if I need one of them I'll let you know."

I walked to the truck where the two bloodhounds voiced a few short barks. Due to their training they knew better, but they were excited. I stroked their ears and talked quietly to them. Ghost had stopped barking. The radio was silent. Della and Cricket were both standing alongside me. Snow was falling, and we were getting wet. We stared silently into the woods where Peter and his big gray dog had gone in. It was very serene, almost surrealistic. Then we heard the muffled crunching of sticks under snow. Peter and Ghost poked out from the woods. It was just the two of them.

"Whatever it was," Peter said, "he was winding the scent, not tracking it. I need to check the map and see what else is back there."

Cricket said, "If you go down the road about fifty yards, there's a two-track that leads back to some summer camps. Otherwise you'd have to go all the way around in order to get in by Joe Hill Hollow. The only thing back there, as far as I know is Joe Hill, the old guy from the hardware store."

Peter nodded, put Ghost back in the truck and said, "You're better than a map. I'll check this side out first, and call Judd. Follow me up to the two-track and we'll see if it's plowed."

Della's cell rang. "It's Foster," she said, tipping the phone away from her mouth. Returning to her caller, "Nothing here either. We're by Peter and checking out some kind of scent the dogs keep getting. We'll keep you posted."

Peter stood at the unplowed side-road. We joined him. "It looks like someone may have been through here on foot before it snowed. But, it wasn't your cousin. The dogs would know. It was probably a rabbit hunter. I have to see if I can find a better scent trail. There are just too many miles of woods to walk in the snow. Maybe I'll try going around the other way. It can't hurt to try."

I gave him back the radio and we said that we were going to try and find more out about the old lady that Hazel had been seen talking to.

As we drove into Ottawa I had an idea, "Cricket, if you were a mixed up crazy lady in an unfamiliar town, where would you go?"

"Why ask me?" she said, then nodded, "Okay, better me than Della. Well, I'd probably go someplace familiar. If I had a clue what was familiar."

"They've checked the estate," Della said.

"All of it? Even my cabin?"

"That, I don't know."

"It would kind of fit," Cricket said, "Mixed up crazy lady, goes outside, starts wandering around, heads to the estate, sees your cabin or your kitties and goes in."

"It's worth a try," Della let out in an exasperated breath of air.

We headed back through Ottawa and toward the big lake.

"Look at that; there are lights on in my cabin. I wonder who's in there."

We pulled into the driveway, and through the window we could see two happy cats, dancing around the living room in the arms of one happy, crazy lady.

"I'll call Blair, and the sheriff and the rescue teams and the cousins, and Foster," Della sighed, "I'm glad she's safe."

Hazel looked out the window, dropped the cats and scampered farther into the cabin.

With phone in hand, Della said, "We better catch her, before she actually does run off."

It was too late. A figure emerged from the back of the cabin; knee deep in snow and heading toward *True North*.

◆◆ 9 ◆◆

The door is always open; the neighbors pay a call...

Once again, getting blanketed in thick snowfall, we cut across the yard and took the trail from my cabin to the big house. The side door was open and we shoved our way in. It was warm inside, but very dark. I handed Cricket my flashlight and stepped away from her and Della to listen. The furnace rumbled far off. There were footsteps crunching on the snow. Cricket flipped on a light switch, the door pushed open behind us and Hazel stood framed in the dark wood.

Before anyone could speak, another door creaked from the far end of the house. "The sun porch," Della said as she grabbed Hazel's hand and snaked her way toward the porch.

I grabbed Cricket's arm and pulled her toward the front entrance, "Let's see if we can head them off."

By the time we unlocked and heaved open the sticking wood door, all we caught were two red tail lights flickering through darkened, snowy trees.

"That house is just too big to maneuver through quickly," Cricket said between breaths.

"Let's check the tracks," I said, unwilling to be out smarted again. Snow was filling in every dip in the landscape. A faint trail led from the side of the estate to the pine row lining the drive where a vehicle had been parked. With only a little light from the small beam of the flashlight it was hard to get the big picture, but it did show boot tracks and tire treads.

"Would it have been too much to have asked for to have a shoe size imprinted in the snow," Cricket said, "Or maybe the year, make and model pressed into the tire tracks?"

"Too much," I said, "but, look over here." I had been shining the light along side the semi-plowed driveway, nearer to where the pines offered a smidgen of protection from the heavy snow.

"This footprint has a distinct boot pattern to it. See how mine makes a zigzag, and yours has a wavy tread? This one has a cross hatch with a sunburst at the toe. It's hard to tell if it was a large woman or a small man. Boots tracks are so deceiving."

Della was beckoning from the door, "Did you see who it was?"

I said to Cricket, as we walked back to the lodge, "Don't say anything in front of Hazel. I'm not sure about her just yet." Cricket agreed, and added, "The only person I am sure of is Della."

After Hazel was retrieved by Blair, Foster deposited back to us and *True North* relocked for the night, we hiked back to my cabin for a hot drink. Foster lit the fire and said, "With all the commotion I haven't heard what '*the vultures*' said about the will?"

Della rested her mug on her knee and gave him the blow by blow of the event. She accounted the scene quite accurately; how each of them had taken turns blaming one another. I remembered Trudi pointing her hot pink fingernails in every direction while Beth Ann stood her ground, from behind her sister. Moira's accusations were sharp edged and cut into character rather than having any viable evidence. Blair had defended herself and Hazel with aloof comments about not having any reason to steal the will, due to the fact she obviously didn't need the money. Hazel agreed with everyone while playing with the paper napkins.

Della left out the fact that she had also accused each of them. There wasn't specific reasoning. She just kept repeating that it wasn't her, so it must have been one of them.

"They all denied it," Della said, "and as far as I could tell, they seemed believable, or at least adamant."

Foster tapped the fireplace poker against the andiron as if it were a pencil, "So, the big question then is, who the biggest liar is."

"Exactly," said Cricket, as she reached for a butterscotch toffee, "and why would someone actually steal the will? I mean, what is there to gain? A long, drawn out court battle doesn't really seem to benefit any of them? So why do it?"

I had been thinking about that, and said, "If Kat was right about hearing Beth Ann and Trudi talking about having a buyer for the place, they might want to keep the property in probate long enough for the rest of the family to get disgusted with the whole process and sell out."

Foster and Cricket jumped in, "Hold on, I think we missed something."

Della explained our conversation at the Pirate's Cove.

"Sell it? To who?" Cricket asked.

Della straightened her back, "We don't know. It doesn't matter. There won't be any selling going on. I'll fight them all the way. The only way they'll sell my place is over my..." She stopped. A hint of uncertainty widened her eyes. "You don't think they're that desperate do you?"

Foster said, "They are selling everything. That's pretty desperate if you ask me. I'll check into it more tomorrow. See if you can get a name of this buyer."

Della leaned back, a little deflated, "We're meeting for lunch tomorrow at the Northern Lights. Today was very unproductive. We thought we'd better take a break. Maybe we'll figure this mess out; if their wounded egos have had time to recuperate."

"Or maybe," Cricket said, "they'll have more time to scheme and refuel. Don't get your hopes up."

Pan was purring softly under my hand. "At least they haven't gotten physical. They must have been taught a few manners. There wasn't any shattering of glass or hurling of silverware today."

"They were brought up wealthy," Della said, "Rich kids learn to be sneaky. Remember the vision you had of the little girl with the broken glasses. That was me. Moira had put cooking oil on the tray's handles."

"How did you know she did it?" Cricket asked.

"She told me. That's how she is; cruel, and proud of herself for being that way. She always felt that I was treated better than her. She took on the attitude of *poor, picked on, neglected Moira.*"

"Would that make her take the will?" I asked.

"If she did," Della said, "she'll try and blame me. Then, eventually, she'll tell me she did it. She'll have to brag, it's in her nature."

"I didn't hear her outright accuse you today," I said.

"It's too soon, she'd have to let the drama stretch out, and tempers get heated so that everyone gets mad at me and she can save the day."

"Maybe she's the crazy one and not Hazel," Cricket said.

"Could be," Della said, "at least Hazel seems happy."

"Does she live with Blair," Foster asked.

Della answered, nodding her head, "She has for her whole grown life, ever since their folks died. Aunt Patsy committed suicide when Hazel was young. Uncle Norville spent all his time at the ship yard, so Blair quit college to take care of her sister."

"Norville was the man Lexi saw," Cricket said, "Maybe there was another woman?"

"I never heard anything about one. But, there could have been. He was going to remarry, but died a month before the wedding of a heart attack, I think. Blair didn't say much about the wedding or the other woman. She's like that, aloof and impersonal."

"I still don't see how any of that would give her a motive," Cricket unwrapped another candy and popped it in her mouth, "and she doesn't need the money."

"I agree," Della said.

Foster looked away from the end of the poker, red hot in the flames. "The lawyer mentioned a copy of the will that your dad had kept. Where would he put it?"

"We could go and check the lodge," Cricket perked up with the idea, "We might even get another visit from the ghost."

"If there had been a first or second visit from a ghost," Foster said.

"How else would you explain it?" she defended herself.

"I won't even get into it," was all he said.

"Good because I don't want to hear your logical explain-it-away theories," she nudged him with her padded wool toe.

Della went to the window facing the big house, "I'd rather go during the day," she said pulling back the linen curtain. "Did we leave a light on over there?"

"No," Foster said, "I checked. When we were leaving I remember turning around and looking. It was dark against the fresh snow. I was thinking how amazing it looked nestled among the virgin pines."

"Foster," Cricket said, "I think Della sees a light."

"Oh, well, there weren't any before."

I nudged Pan off my lap, "Here we go, back out into the cold, dark, snowy night."

Cricket had her boots on, jacket zipped and was clapping her mittens before I had even un-nestled from my blanket. "Calm down," I said, "ghosts don't need lights."

The padded, chipper sounds stopped, "Oh," she said, utterly disappointed, "It must be a person."

♦♦ **10** ♦♦

Oh, there's no place like home for the holidays...

I awoke the next day with bright sunlight streaming through my bedroom window and two hungry cats pawing at my quilt. As I lay there letting the sleep leave my eyes, something dawned on me for the first time. If the estate sold I would lose my little cabin. This is where the cats and I have called home. There wouldn't be the old fashioned pine walls and ceiling that greeted me each morning and comforted me each night with their warm golden tones. The cozy kitchen, the stone fireplace and pale braided rug would belong to someone else. I grabbed my little girl cat, Pixie, looked her in the face, and said; "I don't want to lose Lake Superior as our back yard. We have to help Della."

Pixie and her brother Pan leaped to the floor as I sprang from my bed. I stopped, bent slightly and groaned. I ached terribly. Last night's events had left their mark on me. The memory was as clear as the bluish bruises on my entire right side. Our midnight jaunt to the estate ended with a crash. After finding the main floor void of intruders, Della and Cricket went to scope out the second story bedrooms. Foster and I drew the short match and were to search the cellar. Dusty light bulbs had cast dim illumination on the stone walls and dirty wooden beams. The furnace had droned out the pattering feet of mice and spiders, thankfully. We searched most of the cobwebbed space when Della called to us from the den. As we made our way back up the wooden stairs, my toe caught on an uneven step. I landed first on my knee, which was now swollen. I had slid down about eight steps, bounced off the stone wall and landed on my hip, which was now very bruised and tender.

After Foster eased me from the floor and brushed off an array of dust clumps, we carefully made our way out of the basement. He insisted we leave immediately and get me back to the cabin. I remember, as I hobbled back home with his help, Della had mentioned that someone had been snooping in the den. Two books, a paperweight and the desk blotter had been moved. The dust covered desktop revealed the unmistakable impressions of the objects. She was sure, that with more time and better light, we'd be able to find fingerprints. Her plan was to head back to the lodge after breakfast.

I made my way toward a hot, morning shower in order to sooth my burning muscles and coax them into helping Della keep her family estate. The shower spray stung at the scrapes. The heat did little to ease the stiffness. I was thankful for my no fuss, straight brown hair. I wouldn't have the mobility to use a blow dryer or curling iron. I did manage to brush my teeth and take a couple aspirin. As I stared into the mirror, I saw more than my sandy complexion, green eyes, elfish ears and petite features. I saw the face that went forth each day into a world it loved; filled with natural beauty in a quaint little Lake Superior town. I saw the heart, or soul, which called this cabin home, where inspiration came as rhythmically as the waves. I felt safe here. My ache was deeper than any bruise. It was over the thought of giving up my haven. I wiped tears off of my cheeks and straightened my skinny frame. Turning to the cats, which were statue straight behind me, "I've got work to do. You guys keep the home fires burning. I'll be back. We're not going to have to move again."

I went to the Lighthouse Inn to pick up Della. Foster met me in the lobby and we went upstairs to the *William Riley* and knocked on the door. A man in his mid-forties, with a trim beard and sporty sweater, answered the door. I stumbled on my words, "Is, umm, Della here?"

"Della?" he said, looking down at me, "No, just me."

The door opened behind us and a familiar voice said, "They switched my room - reservation issues."

With a roguish smile, the new occupant of the *Riley* shut the door.

Della motioned us in to the *Nicholas Wesley*. "I like this room. I've been reading the maps and log entries. There's an enchanting view of Ottawa from the window."

We walked over to see for ourselves. I pushed aside the flowing draperies. A snow covered village lay nestled among pines and rolling hills. Foster had rested his chin on the top of my head and said, "I have to bring my camera up here. This is awesome."

Della laughed while lifting her deep green cape off of an ebony chest, and said "It's also a lot warmer than the other room. And, as far as I can tell, it's not haunted either."

Scanning the room I said, "This room is more ornate than the other one."

Foster read from a wall plaque, "*Nicholas Wesley had an easier life than many of the lighthouse keepers due to the fact that the import trade was expanding. Therefore, during the 1920s he had many more luxuries than his predecessors. Navigational techniques were also advancing. Wesley lived a long and prosperous life in Ottawa.*"

While running a mitten along the velvety coverlet, I said, "It's refreshing to hear a story about Lake Superior without storms and hardships. I'm glad someone had a good life."

Foster wrapped his arm around me, "There's a lot of happily-ever-after going on. But, people like to repeat the tales of dread. Those hold an audience. It's human nature. Besides, if nothing terrible happened how would men be able demonstrate their bravery?"

I pushed out from under his arm and batted my eyelashes at him, "Oh yes, rescuing maidens and fighting sea dragons."

As he chivalrously held the door for us he said, "Or protecting friends from rabid relatives, deteriorating staircases and grimy ghosts."

We bantered lightly all the way to the Shipwreck Café where we were to meet Cricket. She was sitting with Judd and Peter. Before we could take off our jackets, she began, "Mabel said a man was in here yesterday asking about *True North.*"

As she opened her mouth to continue, the door jingled. Hot-pink Trudi flashed through followed by Beth Ann, Blair and Hazel. I was glad that the café was filled with weekend snowmobilers, skiers and other visitors so that there was no room to pull tables together for them to join us. They clashed with the Christmas cheer just by their presence. Except for Hazel who wore a bright red coat with a sparkling reindeer pin fastened to the lapel. Blair and Beth Ann nodded toward our table. Hazel beamed us a smile and a feathery wave.

Mabel's sister Pearl brought menus, leaned in close between Della and Judd, and said, "The town's a buzz about your place Ms. True. There's been a man in town asking a lot of questions. He was talking to Bob McMahon about the possibility of rezoning the property as commercial. He said he'd been speaking with the owners about purchasing it and turning it into a recreational area with an indoor pool, convention facilities, a full size golf course and even mini-golf. The town is quite excited."

"Who is he," Cricket whispered. She shrugged and continued pouring her rounds of coffee.

"That's the same story Mabel told me," Cricket said.

"I think my uncle was talking to Aunt Bette about that this morning," Foster said, "Without caffeine I was a little sluggish, sorry. I think I heard him mention Minneapolis. Maybe that's where he's from."

Della was very quiet. The sheriff looked at her and said, "I heard the rumor, too. It seems that he wants to attend the next town meeting about his proposal."

* * *

The door jingled. I tried to turn but my aching body refused. Della told me that the man from the doorway of the *William Riley* had just entered. He scanned the room and then angled his tall frame through the tables and sat with the cousins.

"That's the man we saw this morning," Foster said, "and he sat with your cousins. I bet he's the guy asking about the estate."

"That's him," Pearl said verifying his assumption. She took our orders; five *Snowbound* specials that consisted of two warm, homemade biscuits, two eggs, a side of sausage gravy and brandied peach sauce. Judd ordered his usual. Peter reminded Pearl to please bring the maple syrup.

"We need to get over to the lodge as soon as we've finished," I said.

"I've got my sister Jana watching the shop today," Cricket said, "she and her friends like to be the Saturday staff. They said it's a great vantage point for discreet boy watching. I had to agree, the shop has an ideal location for scoping out the town. So, I'm free all day to help in any way."

Della looked around, mostly toward the table where her cousins were sitting. The clanking of breakfast ware, friendly chatting and holiday music seemed to assure her she could speak, "I want to get back to the den and see if we can figure out who was there last night rummaging through my dad's desk."

"Was someone in the lodge last night?" Peter asked. She explained how we'd gone to the lodge after locating Hazel because we thought she had run from Lexi's to the big house.

She continued, "Well, it wasn't Hazel. She had followed us. Someone else had been by Lexi's. We didn't see who it was. They had left the big house by way of the sun porch door as we were coming in the side entrance. There were only taillights in the woods."

I waited a breath to be sure Della had finished, and added, "There were tracks in the snow, tire treads and boot prints. So, we're keeping our eyes open, for a boot print with a cross hatched pattern with a sunburst at the toe."

"Then, we went back to Lexi's and had some hot cider and cookies," Cricket said.

Foster took his turn at the story, "Della saw a light on at the lodge again. So, we went back over there."

"The place was empty," Della said, "we searched top to bottom, and that's when Lexi fell down the steps and I found things moved on my dad's desk."

Peter and Judd looked back and forth as we spoke and said, "You've been busy."

"Could you fix that step today," Della asked, "I'd hate for anyone else to get hurt."

Peter smiled at her while soaking up syrup on his plate. He mentioned that he had some other fixes to do at the house and that he'd follow us over there.

Before leaving, Della went over to her cousins, "I'll meet you for lunch at the Northern Lights?"

Blair, turning toward Della, flinched and rubbed her shoulder. "Is something wrong, dear?" Della asked.

"It must have been that awful, hard mattress. I'm not use to sleeping anywhere but at home."

Hazel, popping a strawberry into her mouth said, "I slept like a kitty."

Blair slowly turned from Hazel back to her cousin, standing patiently before her, eyeing the stranger seated at the table. Finally she said, "I'd like to introduce you to Mr. William Barrymore. He's a friend of Beth Ann and Trudi from the Twin Cities area."

He rose politely and moved his over six foot tall, well trimmed and trained body to within a foot of Della. She didn't back away. He held out his hand nearly jabbing her in the jacket and said, "It's Bartison, William Bartison, and it's nice to meet you."

She placed the butt of her hand between her breasts, grasped his hand and as she shook it moved the man back out of her space. "Mr. Bartison, what brings you to Ottawa?"

"A little pleasure and a little business; I like to mix them together whenever I can."

Trudi jumped up from her chair, tucked her fluffy, lime, chenille arm into Bartison's and said, "He's here to see me."

"That's nice," said Della, "Maybe he'd like to join us later for a drink at the Pirate's Cove."

"That would be wonderful," Bartison said.

Trudi squeezed at his arm and said, "We had plans later, remember?"

"It can wait. Shall we make it seven?" he said fixating his stare at Della.

"Perfect." she replied, then looking toward Blair, "You could use a rub made from comfrey, rosemary and tea tree for your stiff neck. It works wonders on aches and pains." She walked toward Peter. Bartison's eyes followed her gait. As she reached her friend, she touched his shoulder, whispered in his ear, "I'll explain later," and pecked a kiss on his cheek.

Peter whispered back to her, "No need," and placed a hand on her waist guiding her toward the café's door.

* * *

Peter followed us to the estate house, as promised. The oak door no longer cracked out our arrival. "You fixed the door," I fanned it back and forth on its oiled hinges, "Even though the beastly thing gave me the shivers, it also warned us when someone was coming in. Now they can sneak up on us."

"Maybe we should hang a big bell on it," Cricket suggested, "but, it would have to be a cow bell to be heard throughout this place. I still can't get over how huge it is."

As we headed for the den, Peter said, "I fixed a few other things, too. There are no more dripping faucets, the latches and locks work on all the doors and the fireplaces are clean and functional."

"Even the one in the den?" Della asked. He nodded.

"I thought the damper had broken?" said Cricket.

"It works just fine," he replied.

"What broke and fell into the ashes?" I asked.

"There was some mortar and a few pebbles in the ashes, but nothing else," Peter walked up to the stone hearth and inspected his work, "I could start a fire for you?"

Della suggested that first, they take a closer look. She squatted down and craned her neck, looking up the chimney.

"Let me do that," Peter said, "you'll get full of soot."

I handed him my pocket flashlight and he aimed its beam up the dark rectangular chasm.

"See anything?" Cricket had leaned in close to him.

"Just the normal chimney stuff, let me try something else. I need a small mirror."

Della rummaged in her oversized, suede purse and retrieved a compact, "Will this work?"

"Perfect," he said taking the square brass powder-compact. He clicked it open, positioned it mirror side up inside the stone enclosure.

As he maneuvered it, angling it from side to side, Cricket said, "I get it. It reflects the outside light shining down the chimney. That's pretty slick."

"It's the best way to see if there's creosote built up on the flue walls," he said, "it appears to be clean and in good shape." He moved the mirror some more, paused and said, "There's light coming from the side of the chimney. That's odd; like a small rectangular hole."

Cricket was now nudging against Peter's head to get a look for herself.

Della said, "Maybe that's were the pieces of loose mortar came from?"

Foster had been standing by my side watching intently. He said, "Does it go through to the outside? Could that be where the gusts of air came from?"

Peter handed Cricket the mirror and went to check it out. She hunched closer to the opening and was wiggling the small case to see up the chimney better. "This really works," she said.

Shifting her eyes away from the mirror's effect, she focused on the small compact. "Della, I love this. It looks antique. The floral engravings are beautiful. Where did you get it?"

"It was my mother's," she said. Without warning a blast of air puffed soot right into Cricket's face. She fell back rubbing her eyes. Foster grabbed her hands, "Don't rub them. You'll go blind."

"No I won't. Will I? Because it's already in my eyes," she said spitting black from her lips. Della had dashed for towels and wash rags.

"Here, let's get your face first." She dabbed around her eyes. Water was leaving gray streaks on her cheeks. Once clean, she proclaimed she was alright and that the soot hadn't actually gotten into her eyes.

"I think it was a sign. Someone is trying to tell us something. One minute, there wasn't even a draft, and then I get a shot in the face," she said peering at the fireplace, from a distance.

I picked up Della's brass heirloom and handed it back to her. Black soot dotted the mirror. As she looked down at it she gasped.

"What is it?" Cricket asked.

Della went ghost-white as she stared at the mirror-face.

Peering at it, I could see an image, and said "It's a boot?"

Della tipped her foot back and angled it so that just her toes were resting on the floor. "My dad," she began, "was often busy with people at the shipyard. So, we devised our own secret signal. He'd bend his leg back, like this," she looked back toward her foot, "and tap the tip of his boot on the ground. It was his way of letting me know he was thinking of me."

"I told you it was a sign," Cricket said, "It had to be from Della's dad. It's very ghostly and it's only been happening here, in the den."

"We really should search for the will," I said. Della agreed but could not take her eyes off the image on her mother's small mirror.

Foster and I began looking along the bookshelves. Cricket joined in. We'd quietly tipped books from their orderly places. We were being as unobtrusive as possible. It felt like I was invading someone's privacy.

Peter came back into the room. "I couldn't find where the opening went. I'd probably have to get on the roof, and there's too much snow for that." He looked at me with a questioning expression, taking notice of how we were gingerly perusing the den shelves and Della was entranced near the fireplace. The room grew silent.

Finally I said, "Della, are you okay with us looking through your father's things?"

She broke away from her thoughts, clicked the small compact shut and said, "What?"

"Is it alright with you if we search for the will?" I repeated.

She looked around the room from shelve to desk. Taking a deep breath, she tucked the mirror in her purse and nodded, "I'll start with the desk, and yes, go ahead and look where ever you'd like. It is important that we find it."

As she went to open a drawer, she moaned, "It's been dusted."

We looked around. The entire place was wiped clean. We talked for a few minutes about who could have polished away the proof. Peter took his leave from the den to work on the hazardous basement stair. He patted my shoulder; he'd been able to tell that I was sore. Della began heaving open desk drawers and leafing through papers one by one.

With more enthusiasm, we spent the next hour searching every binding, file folder, furniture cushion and wood crevice in the room. No one found any legal papers. Cricket held a stack of photos. Foster had found some computer discs with years written on them in heavy black marker. Della had a set of keys. My treasures consisted of a child's flip flop, a book of matches, a button and a hand full of coins.

"It's not much," Foster said, "but maybe something here holds a clue. I'll see what's on these discs when I get back to the newspaper office."

"Most of the keys," Della said while flipping them along a big metal ring, one at a time, "look like house or car keys, except this one. Maybe we can find out what it unlocks." She added them to the contents of her purse.

Cricket was studying the photos, "I wish they were in color. It's hard to find a blue dress in a black and white photo."

I held up my findings and said, "I can buy coffee."

* * *

Instead, Foster and I put a pot on to perk in the kitchen while Cricket and Della looked through the snapshots. We sat at the table. Peter had followed the scent of brewed *Holiday Blend* and joined us. Sunlight on snow made the morning feel like Christmas, even without a single wreath on a door or mistletoe from a wooden casing.

Cricket handed me one of the photos, "This looks like Lyda."

I agreed, and as Della leaned over my shoulder, said, "It's her mother, Meredith."

"She's pretty," I said, "Lyda told me yesterday that you and she had played together as kids."

Della smiled, "We both loved to be on the beach. We built sandcastles and picked stones. I liked agates; she liked beach glass; *fairy tears* she'd call them."

"Lyda doesn't talk about her mother very much," I said looking at the photo, "and I didn't notice any pictures of her at the Northern Lights. Maybe she'd like this?"

"Take it with you," Della said, "I'd like her to have it."

I tucked it into my vest pocket and asked, "Should we check out anyplace else today?"

"Like the attic?" Cricket said as she began stacking the photos quickly onto a neat pile.

"I've got about an hour before meeting the family for lunch," Della looked at her silver watch, "If we split up we should be able to do the second floor."

Peter followed us upstairs with his tool belt. He was not going to participate in the search; that was for his dogs. He had work to do.

"Where is the attic?" I asked. Della led us into the children's bedroom and pointed to a hatch in the ceiling, "It has hidden stairs," she said. Foster reached for the pull cord and the door swung open. Ladder style steps unfolded and we stared upward as cold air descended into the room. Foster bounced his weight on a wood rung to see how sturdy the expandable staircase was. Grabbing onto two thin railings, he climbed about halfway up. He swung his arm in a large circle above his head until he found a string. Giving it a pull, a faint shaft of light filtered down through the rectangular opening in the ceiling.

"Wow," was all Foster said.

"What," said Cricket, "what do you see?" She moved closer and looked up toward the opening and then flinched, took a step back and lowered her eyes.

"Afraid a dust ghost will fly from the attic," I asked. She nodded. We laughed

"You have to check this out," he said while climbing the remainder of the rungs until he could perch on the attic floor. I followed slowly upward into the cold. As my head crested the opening I saw it, too. Everything in the attic, from brass bed to floppy hat was covered in thick hoarfrost. Delicate ice patterns covered every surface. Jack Frost had painted toys and furniture, vases and mirrors. Even the floor and rafters were textured in white ice. I moved carefully back down the ladder so that Della and Cricket could take turns looking at the frosty masterpiece. Even Peter had to take a peek. Foster asked if I'd get his camera from the SUV. I brought it to him and he took dozens of digital exposures.

Della asked if I was sore today from my fall. When I told her that that I was, she offered to bring me some herbal ointment she had at the Inn. She then mentioned that Blair had complained of stiffness this morning.

"Maybe she was in here last night and had also tripped on that loose step," Cricket said. We surmised that it was her, but didn't have any proof, or any reason to confront her about it.

"She does have the right to be here," Della said, "I'm not happy about it, but it's a fact."

Unconsciously rubbing at my sore, lower back, I said, "I keep wondering why any of them are snooping around. There must be a reason behind it."

No one answered. The thought hung in the air like the chill from the attic.

After repositioning the spring loaded door, we each took a room and checked dresser drawers, closets and mattresses. There was nothing. I met Foster in the master bedroom and whispered, "We'll have to come back without Peter. I found a couple things that I'd like to get a *feel* for."

Della had to leave for her family meeting. Foster wanted to do some research on Mr. Bartison and check the newly found computer discs. Cricket had to check on her sister at Superior Sweets. Peter went to meet Judd at the café. I decided to take the opportunity to work on Holly Fest. Leaving the estate we made plans to meet later. Glancing back, my gaze rose toward the attic window. Icy lace pictures were painted on the square panes of glass. I imagined the True girls playing dress-up in the summer attic while dreaming of having gala parties like their parents were hosting downstairs.

◆◆ **11** ◆◆

Deck the halls with boughs of holly...

Holly Fest was be in one week. Besides being on the decorating committee, I had offered to assist Priscilla Farmington, the festival coordinator. As the Ottawa Historical Museum director, Priscilla was very organized, meticulous and dependable. Her short coming, as she earnestly acknowledged, was in the field of creativity. Being that I made my living as an artist, she gladly accepted my help. I called Priscilla and we went over her checklist of preparations.

Leslie Walsh, owner of Wildflower Gifts, would be gathering Santa's gifts for the children. Fern and Forrest had ordered the holly and poinsettias. Mabel and Herb would have the food ready for the dinner including sliced turkey, venison barbeque and potato sausage. Lyda and Vivian's menu consisted of a half dozen side dishes. Cricket would whip together the desserts.

Priscilla continued with her party list by saying that Cricket's parents at the Two Loons Saloon would be providing the refreshments including a festive punch. A variety of foods, fireworks, Christmas decorations and party supplies were being donated by the families of Voyageur Enterprises.

When she asked about entertainment for the day, I told her that the music would be handled by the Loose Moose. They have a number of local musicians lined up for the evening. Thorny will be there with the Old Timers Band, complete with fiddle, mandolin and accordion. Also, the high school choir will be singing carols.

I asked if Joe Hill was bringing in his team of horses and the sleigh. She assured me that he was, and that he'd be delivering Santa promptly at three o'clock. I hoped that Thomas Greene would be there again this year telling Native American stories to the children. I noted that Peter and Judd had been gathering the wood for the bonfire. Foster was in charge of taking pictures. I'd begin decorating on Wednesday at the Community Center. We needed to get a hold of Bette and Bob McMahon about the games. She offered to meet me on Wednesday for any final arrangements. We hung up and I continued to jot a few notes along with a complete list of decorations.

The more I worked on the Holly Fest, the more excited I got. My family would be coming, along with many of the other out-of-town relatives of those living in Ottawa. I wished that Della and her family could resolve their differences before Holly Fest. It would be nice if they could join in and enjoy the party.

At the window of my cabin, I stared out over the frozen lake with patches of dark ice. Winter didn't offer the rhythm of the waves and rich blues of the water. Instead, there were the threatening cracks as the ice shifted and the endless miles of cold white. An updraft of wind swirled a sheen of snow over the smooth drifts glistening in the late afternoon sun. Living along Lake Superior was magnificent and ever changing. I liked it here. I did not want to move.

I wondered if the conversation at the Northern Lights was being as harsh as the landscape outside my window. Would the family really sell? Could Della prevent it? I needed to talk with Cricket and Foster. We needed a plan. We had to help her.

The *closed* sign was turned when I pulled up in front of Superior Sweets. I walked the narrow path shoveled to Cricket's back door entrance to her attached apartment. Her lapis-blue door was fashioned with a heavy, brass door knocker in the shape of a butterfly. The sign below it said *Rattle my wings and Flutter on in!* Her witty sayings, posted throughout her home and shop, always made me smile. I rattled the wings and fluttered on in. Licorice, her little black kitten, met me at the door. Cricket yelled from the other room, "Who is it?"

"Heikka Lunta, your local snow goddess" I hollered in response while taking off my boots, coat, hat and mittens, "I'm here to save Della's Christmas; and my home."

She poked her head around the corner and said, "I'm not sure what you're talking about? But it sounds like you're on a mission"

"I am. And, I need your help."

She poured coffee into two mismatched earthenware mugs. With a plate of rosette cookies between us and cats on our laps we began tossing ideas into an invisible pot to see what we could brew up. Foster must have smelled the cookies. He fluttered on in and also began adding to the pot of schemes.

After about an hour we had a kettle full of plans stewing that we wanted to share with Della. Foster also had some information about Bartison, and the contents of the diskettes we'd found in the den. We were all dying to hear about Della's family meeting.

"I downloaded those photos from the attic," Foster said while finishing the last Christmas cookie, "They're amazing. I grabbed the laptop, so that I could show you."

"I can't wait to see them," I said while getting re-dressed for the outside weather. Cricket was rustling around in her cozy little kitchen, and then scurried into the living room. She appeared with a back pack and said, "Let's go and see what that big house has to tell us tonight."

Foster and I looked at her inquisitively. She waved us out the door without an explanation.

We were seated at the big oak table under an antlered chandelier in *True North* when Della arrived. She plopped her purse on the table and her body into a chair, and said, "That was exhausting."

"What happened? What did they say?" Cricket began drilling her.

"I need to relax a minute before getting into it," she said picking at the little sandwiches Cricket had brought with her and had neatly arranged on a Jadeite plate from the china hutch.

"Tell me about your day first."

Foster began with his findings on William Bartison explaining that he was a real estate broker from Minneapolis who appeared to focus on wealthy clients. "His website shows elaborate waterfront properties and million dollar vacation homes. The interesting thing, that I noticed, was that he seemed to deal strictly in residential properties. There wasn't any mention of commercial investments."

As I was pouring coffee, I said, "Isn't he saying, to the town, that he has buyers who want to make this into a *public* recreation area?"

"That's what I understood," Cricket said.

Della took a sip a coffee and said, "That's what Trudi is saying, too."

"I did some more searches," Foster added, "and it appears that Mr. Bartison is engaged, and not to your cousin."

"That's interesting," Cricket said, "he was also making eyes at Della."

"He probably figures it's a way to seal his business deal," I said, "What a slimeball."

Della explained how Trudi and Beth Ann tried to convince her that this was the best plan. She said how they had a well-rehearsed script which they had been selling to the Ottawa business people and anyone who would listen.

"What were they saying? "Cricket asked.

"They said that the town would profit from the tourism generated by the facility. There would also be jobs and a greater tax base. They also made sure to mention to the town's people that they would have full use of the complex at a discount resident rate. They proceeded to persuade me by saying, that the sale of the property would be better for Ottawa as a whole, rather than if we selfishly kept it in the family for personal use only."

"Who are *they*?" I asked.

"Trudi was doing most of the talking, Beth Ann nodded a lot. When it became too technical for Trudi to explain, Blair would interject details."

"Why is Blair siding with Trudi and Beth Ann to sell?" Foster said, "She has plenty of money, or at least that's what she boasts on her meager website."

"I'm not sure," Della replied, "it has me puzzled."

"What did Moira have to say about selling?" I asked.

Della was shaking her head, "She said that it didn't matter to her. She acted completely disinterested."

"I'm curious about the will; what did they say?" Cricket asked.

Della explained that they each acted as if she was making it up. They said to ask the lawyer to look again. Moira said to check with the register of deeds and see whose name the property was in. "I actually thought that was a good suggestion."

We all agreed. Della said that she'd do that first thing Monday morning and added, "The cousins got a little nervous about checking on the deed but, they tried to hide their discomfort. Blair is a better actress than Trudi or Beth Ann."

Della picked at another little sandwich, and shyly said, "I got very upset with them, and I may have said a few unintentional things."

Cricket asked, "What do you mean?"

"Well," she started, with her face blushing, "I told them that my friends had checked into their finances and found them to be lacking, and that *we* were going to save *True North* from being sold. I also told them that *we'd* find dad's will and then everything would be cleared up." She stopped, took a breath and said, "I also accused them of sneaking around the estate. They reminded me that they had every right to be there." She sighed. "It was not a pleasant afternoon."

I had never seen Della so discouraged and she actually acted beaten. I looked at Cricket and Foster and said to our distraught friend, "We have some ideas."

♦♦ 12 ♦♦

He's making a list and checking it twice...

"There are a few things we need to do," Cricket said, "First we have to find out who's been in your dad's den."

Foster smoothed back his thick red bangs, "I can get sensor cameras. A guy I interviewed uses them for hunting to see what animals are coming into his bait piles. They will work perfect for catching a rat in the act."

"Next," Cricket continued, "we need to find out more about Mr. William Bartison. I smell trouble whenever he's near. I think he's not an honest man."

I joined in, "I'm going to make some inquiries about real estate, talk to his staff, while he's still in Ottawa. Then after we find out more information we'll deal with Trudi and the knowledge of the fiancé."

Cricket took the lead, "We need you to play along with him a little. Pretend to be interested in him. We need him to stay in Ottawa until we know more."

Before Della could object, I said, "Cricket is going to go to the town council, and Foster will speak with his uncle. We have to convince them not to back this sale until all the facts have been verified."

Foster spoke, "It's important we find the will, so Lexi and I are going to spend some time here while she does her *thing*. There has to be more clues."

Della looked around the room nervously, "I keep getting a weird feeling that someone is listening."

Foster began searching around window sills and door frames. He checked the fireplace mantel and the baseboards. Cricket couldn't sit still. She paced, as if sniffing the air. She turned sharply, walked directly to the china hutch and opened the glass door.

"Earlier, I sensed something out of place," she said while studying the glassware, "Everything is very orderly except this teapot. The handle is turned." She reached in and gently removed it as Foster came to her side. He removed a small wireless recording device, "I wonder if there are more of these bugs in the house?"

We paraded around the mansion from room to room while Cricket studied them for items out of place. In the great room there was a vase moved from its dusty position, leaving a shiny half circle of wood exposed. Behind it, another wireless recorder was found. In the den, books would have made a great cover, but instead the small machine was hiding between a ship in a bottle and a brass statue of a sailing boat which had been turned at an odd angle. After a full search of the second floor we held only three of the high-tech devices.

Foster inspected the recorders, "I'll have to use the computer to see what's on the memory cards." He looked up and slapped at his head, "Oh, I almost forgot, I opened the discs with the years marked on them. It was mostly diagrams of ships along with spec sheets. There were a few financial statements, but nothing that seemed unusual."

"Why would my dad have had that information here?" Della asked. Foster couldn't answer that. "The last disc had an appointment schedule on it, as well as business contacts. There was also some odd entry data. I printed it out for you to look at."

As we returned to the dining room, Cricket pulled a blue velvet pouch from her knapsack. "I think Cricket wants to do a reading" I said taking a seat.

She placed the deck of oversized cards on the table. I admired their smooth surface, ornately painted with golden stars and silver moons on a midnight background. "Who are you doing the reading for?" I asked.

"Della," she said. Cricket began shuffling the cards. Her hands moved in a well practiced motion laying card over card. Looking at her frazzled friend she said, "I have a feeling, that you have some questions."

"Lots of them," Della said and took the cards from Cricket.

Foster sat down next to me and said, "There are a lot of things that need answering. Maybe we can get a line on that will."

* * *

"Don't get carried away," Cricket said, "they aren't going to say *pull out the last book on the big shelf and you'll find the papers you want.*"

He laughed, "I know, but I can wish."

"All you're going to get is the wishing," Cricket said as Della handed her back the well shuffled tarot deck.

"Tonight, I think we need double cards," Cricket began laying out two cards at a time.

"These are the past." Then she laid two more beneath them, saying that they represented the present and two more below those for the future. The golden stars and silver moons glimmered in the light from the chandelier.

Cricket tipped her head and said, "It's interesting. I didn't really think of it but, the cards resemble the six cousins; the three sets of two sisters."

"I wonder if that's what Della's question is about," I said and nudged my friend as she sat quietly looking at the cards Cricket had laid out. Della looked worn out. Even her usually well kept appearance, complete with green wool blazer and designer stone jewelry, couldn't hide her muddled spirit.

Cricket took a deep breath and turned over the top two cards. "In the past position the cards are the King of Pentacles and the Jack of Swords." She looked at Della, "Two men have made a big impact in your past it seems. I'd say that the King is your dad, but the Jack is someone who has hurt you very deeply."

Della was silent and motionless. I looked at her for some sort of response and there was none.

Cricket noticed this too, so she continued by turning over the cards of the present, "I see here that we have the Temperance card and the Five of Cups." She paused, studying the cards.

"What does it mean? " Foster asked.

She studied them a little longer and said, "Balance is needed. Obviously, Della has been emotionally and physically drained. Grief can take its toll on a person."

She reached over and touched Della's hand, "It's time to take care of you. Temper your need to control this situation with letting it go. Also, the Five is asking; *do you see your cup half empty of half full?*"

Della continued to stare at the cards, entranced in her thoughts.

Cricket turned over the last two cards and began to laugh. Her chuckles turned to snorts. Della broke from her concentration to stare at Cricket, "How do you find this funny? My whole life is falling apart and you find this funny?"

"I'm sorry," Cricket said still laughing, "I'm not doing it, you are."

"What do you mean?" Della said.

"Look at the card."

Della focused on the card; so did I. It was of a woman dancing on stones on the water, except it wasn't stones, it was heads bobbing in a lake. I tried not to laugh, but a giggle snuck out. Della put her finger on the card and counted the heads; one, two, three, four, five. "Oh my," she said.

"Looks like there are a few women who can hardly keep their heads above water thanks to you," Cricket said.

"I don't want to do this to them," Della said, still unable to see the humor.

"Della," Cricket looked her in the eyes, "You aren't doing it to them. They've brought this all on themselves."

Foster poked at the card, "It's not like you're drowning them."

Della chuckled, finally, "After the way they've been acting, I wouldn't mind seeing them up to their necks in their own deceptions." We nodded in agreement.

"What's the last card?" Foster asked.

"Well," she said, "It seems that there's one more hurdle to cross. It's the Tower."

"It's burning and crumbling to the ground. Does it mean that the estate is going to be torn down?" Foster asked, looking horrified.

"Not at all," I told him, "It's just saying that something is going to change and it's inevitable."

Della sat back in her chair and sighed. Cricket said, "Don't forget when it's all falling apart, it's actually falling together."

"That's a lot to take in," Foster said, "I'm going to let you ladies talk and go get some food. This made me hungry."

"Everything makes him hungry," I said as he left the room. Then I asked Della about the Jack of Swords.

She hesitated and then leaned in toward the table, "There are things that happened in this house. Things that I'd like to forget, but they obviously keep coming back to haunt me."

Cricket and I looked at her, "Do you want to talk about them?" I asked.

"What kind of things?" Cricket prodded, "We've all had bad stuff happen to us. Woman should talk about it. It's how we help each other through it."

Foster was rattling around in the kitchen. Della said, "I know. But, it was a long time ago and now is not the time. It was good that the cards reminded me that all the memories in *True North* were not all sunny and sweet for me or for them."

She looked back up at us, "That's why I had to spend a few minutes alone in the house the other night. It was the first time I've been back since I was a teenager. I had to face my demons alone."

"No you don't," we both said. She smiled. We could hear Foster heading back toward the dining room.

Della said, "Maybe we can talk more another night."

As Foster came through the door Della said, "It's time to go to the Pirate's Cove and meet Mr. Bartison. I have some schmoozing to do."

As we had decided, Foster and I would stay at the estate while Della and Cricket went on the man mission. Cricket was delighted and hopeful that her snowmobile friends would be there, too.

♦♦ **13** ♦♦

Do you remember the one you used to know...
"Lexi, before we go rummaging through the mansion, I want to show you those photos from the attic." Foster booted up his laptop. He was an excellent photographer. Besides taking pictures for the newspaper he was working on a photo journal called *Raw Emotions*. I'd seen many of the black and white images he'd taken of people. Each depicted the wide range of human expression. He had a talent for capturing a person's natural essence. The photos were moving and dynamic.

Frame-by-frame images recreated the icy scene in the attic. They were impressive.

"These are beautiful. I'm not sure if I like them better in color or gray-scaled. Both versions hold distinct qualities."

The color photos captured and singled out the items frozen in time with the frost muting the details. The black and white images presented an eerie rendition of the past trapped in ice. As he clicked through the two dozen shots, something caught my eye, "Back up to the color version of that photo."

Racks of clothing were positioned behind a large oval mirror. "They look like they're shrouded., I'd love to go back up there." Foster suggested we waited until daytime when we'd have more light. I agreed.

He began to shut down the computer when I noticed a file folder with my initials on it. Before I could inquire about it the screen went black and he said, "Are you ready for our expedition into the past. I'm rather curious to see if you'll get any mysterious feelings from this place."

"Me too," I said and removed my special-made gloves. They peeled from my hands like a layer of skin. Years ago I had them made. It was the only way I could stay *in-touch* with the world around me without picking up on thoughts and memories left on objects my hands came in contact with. I don't have to wear them all the time, but I keep them in my pocket for safe measure. In winter, as a bonus, they also help keep my hands warm.

We began walking through the big house. "Where do you want to start?" Foster asked. Before I could answer, he said, "How about the den?"

"I wish we could have gotten here sooner. We've touched everything," I said looking around for something that might hold a clue to the whereabouts of the will. I scanned the book shelf, the desk, the fireplace mantel and the furniture. Foster watched.

Finally, I said, "Any item is as good as the next," and reached for *Superior Hauntings.*

My eyes were burning as I stared at the cover of the book I began leafing through its pages searching for something. I felt desperate. There was faint conversation around me. I was shaking the book with great ferocity. My thoughts were angry; Where is it? I know it's here. Looking up I saw who was in the den with me.

I broke from the vision by laying the book on the desk and said, "That was weird."

Foster was waiting for my explanation, "What did you see?"

"I saw you and Cricket; and myself. That has never happened before. It was from the other night when we were here and Della had been looking through the book. It was like déjà vu."

I picked through more items in the den; a statue on the mantel, other books, paperwork on the desk and furniture. The same thing happened every time. There weren't any images from years ago; instead they were from days ago. "It's hopeless, let's go to another room."

The great room had been dusted. It would be another lost cause. Foster decided that the second floor held more possibilities. I kept my hand from the stair rail. As we reached the top landing, Foster spun in a circle with his arm outstretched like an arrow. He stopped, pointed and said, "Let's start there." It was the kid's room.

As we entered, the scent of musty stuffed toys mingled with talcum powder. Along the far right hand wall, a row of dolls, fluffy bears and miniature furniture was randomly stacked among books and games.

Two twin beds, draped in yellow lace coverlets, were directly ahead with a window between them. Lying with their heads resting on the pillows were two very different dolls. One was dressed in bright red gingham and wore a white eyelet lace apron. She had blonde hair and was neat and tidy. The other had three layers of dresses tugged over its worn body. The top layer was a bright green and gold print, probably from the seventies. Its hair was matted, that is, where it was still attached to the soft, plastic head.

"I think these dolls will be a good place to start," I told Foster who was snooping through closets and dressers.

While sitting on the bed, I took the tattered doll in my hands.

It was immediately sunny and warm in the room. The curtains were blowing in from the open window and brushed my hair. I could feel myself reaching up and brushing a tear from my cheek. My stomach ached and I began to rock and hum. I knew the tune, it was a familiar soft lullaby, not one a child would know but someone older. I reached down to fix my sandal, my foot was sunburned; my ankle was scraped. There was music playing in the background, it was the tune I was humming. I clutched the baby doll close to my chest and was twisting my fingers in its hair. Mary Jane is a good girl I was say-

*ing softly, She didn't do anything wrong. I heard a woman
calling. As I laid the baby on the bed I fixed her yellow flow-
ered dress and crossed her tiny feet.*

That was it. It was over. Foster came and sat by me, "Anything?" he asked. I told him what I'd seen, he jotted notes in a
little spiral book he had handy in his pocket; always the good
reporter. I moved to the other bed, took a deep breath and
picked up the other doll. After sitting on the bed for about five
minutes, I explained to Foster what I'd seen.

"The rows of toys were in front of me; lined up pretty
much like we see them now. I turned, saw the beds neatly
made and walked to the window. When I pushed aside the
sheer curtain to look out the window, I had to bend down to
see out through the lower pane."

"So, you must have been about this tall," he gestured with
his hands to about five feet.

"That seems right," I said, and continued, "The Lake was
deep blue and the trees were beginning to turn yellow. I
looked up and down the beach. I felt anxious. Then, I saw a
person peering from behind the bushes close to the shoreline."

"Could you see who it was?" he asked.

"Just that it was a man, medium height and build," I answered, "He waved, and I waved back. I could see my reflec-
tion in the glass; I was smiling." Foster wanted to know if I
could remember what I looked like. The only thing I recalled
was that I was a young teen with a shiny barrette holding back
wavy hair. I told him, that as the teenager, I laid the doll on the
bed and it was over.

"This isn't really helpful," Foster said, "It's actually rais-
ing more questions."

I agreed.

He looked at his notes, and said, "The girls could be Della
and Moira, or any of the sets of cousins. Or, for that matter, it
could be any of them at any point in time." He closed the little
book and said, "It's very frustrating Lexi."

I nodded again, then added, "Maybe Della can help. But, even if she does know who the girls were it doesn't really help with finding the will."

"I feel like we're digging into years of this family's life without really getting a bigger picture," Foster said. I told him that I felt the same way, that's why I was hoping that this excursion would help. We discussed the fact there were too many people who had been a part of this estate. Beside the owners and their families, there was house staff, friends and many people from Ottawa who had all been in *True North* touching things.

"This is futile," I said pulling on my tight skinned gloves.

We went to the window and looked out over Lake Superior. The night was clear and cold as a white moon cast subtle light over the reflective snow. Foster scraped his fingernail against the leafy ice patterns on the window leaving a sharp trail cut through the frost. "There is so much we don't know. To gather and sort through all the historic information would take an extremely long time. Even then, how would we find out what was relevant?"

We heard a noise downstairs. We hollered hello. No one answered. Foster went to the top of the stairs and yelled again. He motioned for me to follow and we moved as quietly as the creaky old stairs would allow. As we reached the bottom stair a door slammed.

"The side entrance," Foster said as we ran from the foyer, across the great room and toward the outside entry on the far side of the kitchen. Before reaching the door Foster slipped. His arms flew up. He caught his elbow against my already sore shoulder sending me sideways against the door frame. I felt my feet giving way beneath me. My hip caught the doorknob before I sank with a thump onto the floor. Foster had fallen backwards, nearly catching his head on the countertop. I realized that the kitchen light had been turned off. We were both groaning. That was a good sign. We were both conscious and alive.

"Are you okay?" he asked.

"I think so. How about you?"

"Let me get the light." He scooted over to the wall and reached up to flick on the switch,

"What did we slip on?"

I reached my hand along the floor. It felt greasy, "I think its oil."

He moved closer to me and we carefully got up. He sniffed his hand, "I think its wax; like floor wax."

We looked at each other and I finally said, "Do you think someone did this on purpose?"

"I don't think it was the cleaning lady."

◆◆ 14 ◆◆

So this is Christmas, what have you done?...

The cats were curled up on a blanket by the Christmas tree. Foster was placing logs in the fireplace while I called Cricket to ask her and Della to stop by my cabin after the Pirate's Cove. When they arrived nearly an hour later, they heaved themselves through the door like giant snowballs, nearly popping the hinges from the old wood.

"You are not going to believe what happened to us?" Cricket said.

I looked at her rather puzzled, and said, "That was supposed to be my line."

As they pulled off boots, jackets and layers of winterwear, Della asked what I had meant, while starting in on her own story, "Someone slashed my tire."

Cricket jumped in, "We had all we could take of Bartison and Trudi so, we decided to leave. Trudi kept talking, even while we suited up and started for the door. As we got into the vehicle, a snowmobiler tapped on the window and told us we had a flat tire. He and his friend offered to change it. Wasn't that nice?" I nodded at her to keep on track and not go off on a man story.

Instead, Della finished, "They told us to wait inside where it was warm."

"How did you know it was slashed?" Foster asked.

"They showed us," Della replied.

"Did they see who did it?" he asked. They both shook their heads and were quiet.

Foster filled in the silence by telling them about our skating accident on the floor of the estate and the elusive visitor. "We cleaned up the mess and went to look for tracks," he said.

"They took a broom and covered their boot prints," I told them, "We couldn't make out anything."

We all agreed that both incidents were obviously premeditated. The only people accounted for during the night were the four of us, Trudi and Bartison. The rest of the clan had been at large. Della repeatedly apologized for getting us involved in something that was becoming dangerous. We assured her that we chose to help. In a moment of truthfulness, I confessed that I had an ulterior motive: my cabin.

We decide to tell the sheriff in the morning and hopefully he would check alibis. We concluded it would be better if he investigated this situation. Accusing Della's family of sabotage and malicious destruction may cause an even bigger uproar.

After cups of hot Toddies and homemade caramel corn were place on the coffee table, I told Della about my encounters in the big house. She said the dolls did not belong to any one person in particular.

"We kept our favorite toys at home so they wouldn't get lost or ruined by the many children playing at *True North.* Moira always liked the doll with the red dress," she said, "Actually; she'd hide it from the other girls. As far as the barrette; Moira had poker-straight hair as a kid. She still does. So, I can't help with that."

Cricket liked my story about seeing my own image in the den. It was unanimous; the *touching*-trip at the lodge was a good idea without good results. Della and Cricket said that their meeting with Mr. Bartison was also a bust.

"We spent more time watching Trudi paw him than we actually had opportunity to drill him for information. She made sure of that," Cricket said, while snagging another handful of nutty caramel corn. "She was making a complete fool of herself."

"We had a nice time chatting with Kat," Della offered, trying to justify the evening out, "And Cricket seemed to find a little pleasure in a few rounds of pool with the snowmobilers."

Cricket giggled, "Hey might as well have a ball while the snow flies."

The following morning I slept in. Later, I found out that all four of us had stayed in bed as long as cats, telephones and bladders would let us. I assumed it was due to shear exhaustion. It was nearly noon when I left the cabin. I had promised Whistler that I'd find Macy's Christmas present. It would be a good day for a road trip to Houghton where I could visit my parents and do some Christmas shopping. Maybe even catch my brother at home.

The sun was shining and the roads were clear. When speaking of roads during the winter in Upper Michigan, *'clear'* was a relative term. Black pavement was visible in four long lanes where tires snaked down each side of the two-lane highways. Winter driving was always a challenge and a four-wheel-drive vehicle a smart investment. It made me wonder again, why Trudi, with her little red sports car, was on the Red

Earth Road. It was one of many things that were as unclear as a Michigan road in December.

After purchasing Whistler's gift for his granddaughter, I found a camera accessory bag for Foster. He had mentioned that even though he liked his field pack, it was too small to hold his extra equipment. I had already found Cricket's present at the Loose Moose. She had fallen in love with a wooden chest inlayed with silver snowflakes over an ornately painted woodland scene. She had said it would make a perfect hope chest; if she ever decided to fall in love again. If not, she said it would be great storage for mittens and scarves. She had a way of being practical while awaiting romance.

Most of my gifts I'd be able to find in Ottawa. I needed to locate a camping set for my niece Kaitlin. At six, she wanted her own tent, sleeping bag and lantern. I would see if they had one at Ottawa Outfitters. I could find something there for my brother, also. My dad liked books, so North Bound Books, which was located in the same building as The Ottawa Ledger, would surely have something he'd like. I'd ask Foster to help me choose a good rock book for my geology professor dad. Mom liked anything that had dogs on it. I'd scope out Voyageur Clothing for something unique for Della; and maybe my sister-in-law, too.

I was going over a mental checklist of other small items I needed for stocking stuffers and secret-Santa gifts when I arrived at my parents' home. I had only spent a few years here at the end of high school, so it didn't hold childhood memories. Renovations had kept my dad busy while mom spent hours on the gardens of herbs, flowers and vegetable. They had taken an older mining house and turned it into a charming north-country foster home for dogs.

Greeting me through the gate were a young, energetic, golden retriever and a whimpering, wriggling, little terrier of sorts. They let me in and jumped, licked and nearly tripped me all the way to the front door. Peering through the huge pine wreath center over the red door's wavy glass panes, I could see my mom, Maggie Marx, hurrying to see what all the barking was about. I opened the door a crack and squeezed in.

She clasped her hands and then reached out and pulled me in for a big hug, "Hi sweetheart; I didn't know you were coming?"

A fluffy, buff colored poodle peeked over the sofa at me with its tail waggling. "How many borders to you have this week?" I asked while rubbing the little pooch's ears.

"Just three," she said.

We talked about Christmas dinner, Kaitlin's kindergarten program and Holly Fest. I told her a little of Della's plight in Ottawa. She filled me in on dad's latest project; building a tub-sized rock garden fountain for the sun porch. My brother, Garrett, was on an official search in the Copper Country for a missing snowmobiler. He wasn't expected home until tomorrow. She assured me she'd let him know I had been here and that I had a surprise for my niece when they came to Ottawa for Holly Fest.

During the first half of the ride home I thought about what I still needed to get done before the weekend. As I got closer to Ottawa, I decided to take the Red Earth Road. The lake drive would be beautiful in the late afternoon. Arrangements had been made for a seven o'clock supper at Cricket's. I had plenty of time to take the scenic route and make a stop at the Mission Point Bakery.

My mind started to wind through the events of the past few days as if following the curves in the road. It moved from images as shadowy as the thick pine forests to answers as untouchable as the lake's far horizon. Occasionally, a sharp edged rock cliff would remind me of eminent danger. When Silver Bay came into sight I saw ice had broke near a river inlet exposing open water. It gave me hope.

By the time I reached the bakery it was closed for the day. There would be no sourdough rolls or cranberry walnut sweet bread for supper. Superior Sweets had delicious treats, but Mission Point had wholesome baked goods that I craved. Both fed my soul.

When I came to the spot where Trudi had went into the ditch I pulled the Explorer to the side of the road. I was about one mile from town, near where Peter had been parked while Ghost searched the woods. *Could that be a coincidence,* I thought. I didn't really believe that. As a rule, there are no coincidences; everything is connected.

What was Trudi's motivation? Why was she out here? The sun was getting low. Most of the snow had been blown from the trees allowing for visibility through the bare, leafless branches. Far off in the distance a faint light flickered. I'd have to ask Cricket if Joe Hill's farm could be seen from the road. I didn't think it would be possible, but the woods can be deceiving.

◆◆ 15 ◆◆

The holly bears a berry, as red as any blood...

Cricket had made a thick pot of venison stew for supper with homemade biscuits. Arriving ahead of Della and Foster, I played with the kitties and then set the table. Cricket told me the theme for the evening was *woods and water.* I chose dishes with pine branches, chickadees, blue swirls and brightly painted fish. I loved perusing through her dishes. Each one was purposefully different. As were the glasses, bowls, silverware, coffee mugs, place mats and napkins. Green, blue, gold and clear crystal glasses were placed by the plates which sat on top of pine and berry designed place mats; each one also different.

Setting up the round oak table was like playing tea party as a kid. It was fun and interesting. The difference was that the food was real and always scrumptious.

Della and Foster arrived minutes apart. "I hope red wine is alright?" she asked placing a bottle of Merlot on the table.

"Red is ideal; it is Christmastime," Cricket replied while placing a salad dressed with raspberry pecan vinaigrette on the table. Mandarin oranges, thimbleberries and dark cherries poked through the mixed greens.

There was a knock on the door, and Della said, "I invited Peter. I hope that was alright?" I scurried for another place setting.

Cricket just chuckled, "That'll be great. I'll only be eating leftovers for two days instead of three." She heaved a large, blue enamelware pot from the stove and placed it in the center of the table. Foster filled a basket with hot biscuits. Food was passed, talk was light and cheery. Cricket had a rule about eating: *Sour words spoil the food –sweet talk sets the mood.*

After the main course; the *woods* part of the theme. Cricket produced the *water* segment of her meal. She passed a tray of miss matched sundae cups filled with a blue gelatin heaped with a frothy topping that looked like snow. "I call it The Winter Blues." It tasted like chilled lemon meringue with a hint of berry. Compliments and sounds of delight moved around the table as if a blues song was being sung as we spooned more of the concoction into our mouths.

Hazelnut coffees were taken into the living room where the cats curled up on Cricket's oversized, old fashioned furniture. Foster explained that he'd been on deadline today and was very busy. He hadn't had time to check on the recorders or search for anything on the Internet. Della had tried to contact the lawyer, but he was out of town; Christmas shopping. She had avoided her cousins.

Peter said that he had taken Della to talk with Judd who said that he'd investigate both the tire slashing and the sabotage at the lodge. "I can't believe Della's family would be so brutal," Peter said, "they're as mean as a pack of badgers."

"There's obviously something more behind all of their ruthless actions," Cricket said.

"What would their motives be," I asked, "other than basic greed?"

Peter, who was sitting comfortably with Bon Bon, the tan Siamese, on his lap, said, "Over the years, I've seen where people get strange notions in their heads for any number of reasons. Most of the time it stems from the fact that they've felt wronged in life." He continued to stroke the cat as we listened. "They've felt gypped out of money, taken advantage of, cheated on, treated unjust by society or some other victim type scenario."

"We do live in a victim orientated society," Della said, "People blame others and don't take responsibility for their own actions."

Foster tipped his head, and said, "So, why do your family members feel victimized? That could lead to a motive."

Cricket passed around small fleecy blankets as she said, "It would probably be more like motives. They all seem to have hatred built up against society, Della and even themselves. I get a feeling that they don't really like who they are; except Hazel."

We tossed each name out and came up with sketchy victim profiles for each of them starting with Moira. As Della had said before, her sister felt neglected as a child. As an adult she had become a social recluse with a protective barrier around her. She seemed to be financially stable. She was married for a short time years ago and then after the divorce never even dated.

Della's face was lined with sadness as she said, "She told me once, that men weren't worth her time. They were all cheaters and immature buffoons. She's worked as a legal secretary for many years. As far as I know she's satisfied with the position and didn't have any other real career aspirations."

"What does she do in her free time?" Cricket asked.

"I'm not really sure. She has a beautiful home in Duluth. She never mentions friends," Della bowed her head, "But, I haven't really stayed in touch with her."

"She's not the nicest person to be around," I said.

So Moira's motive would be purely spite, we decided.

Blair was even more financially well-heeled than Moira. It was obvious that she played martyr as caretaker of her crazy sister. That was a definite mark on the injustice side of the list. She never married, again because of Hazel. Any real life she may have wanted for herself was given up.

"Blair seems to really care about Hazel," I said. We all agreed to that.

Peter said, "Have you ever know someone who had to care for an elderly parent, or sick relative? They love them, but they still often feel resentful."

"Blair's motive would come from the fact that she felt cheated," Foster said, "What about Hazel? Could she be responsible at all?"

It was unanimous that Hazel didn't have the mental capacity, even if she had a motive.

"Unless," Cricket said, "The craziness is an act."

"Or," Foster added, "There's a dark unconscionable side to her craziness."

We all looked at Della as she said, "Anything's possible. I really can't say one way or another"

Cricket poured coffee and brought in cookies for the next round; Beth Ann and Trudi.

We started with the older sister. Beth Ann seemed to need money. She oozed *poor me* from every wringing hand movement to simpering comment. Her husband had left her for a farmer's daughter who had inherited both money and land,

Della explained. "As long as I can remember, she's always walked in Trudi's shadow."

"I think she's sneakier that we're giving her credit for, and smarter," Cricket said while offering a bit of cookie to her little black cat.

Della thought about that for a moment, and said, "Possibly, she went to college and received a degree in hotel management, and then never did anything with it. Trudi wanted to open a boutique. It drained a lot of their funds and in the end they went bankrupt."

"I think Beth Ann has a mountain of motives," Cricket said.

Trudi was the last badger to be analyzed. She had the hiss, growl and bite. The only thing lacking was the brains. Was she truly like a badger, having an escape hole ready if danger threatened? We didn't think so. We guessed that she'd get caught if trapped. She made it clear that she needed money, deserved a better life and it was everyone else's fault that she didn't have these things. Cricket said that she probably even blamed Beth Ann.

As we thought over our assumptions, we surmised that Trudi, Beth Ann and Blair had the most motives. Moira's motive was singular but fierce. Hazel was off the hook or the wildcard. After hashing over some basic information it was clear that Della's family had some issues, but it didn't actually get us any closer to finding out who took the will.

Peter summed up our discussion by saying, "There are possibly four women who feel wronged, and one who can't remember if she's been wronged. The motives are foggy, but they're present. Now, who had the means to take the documents and put you in danger?"

"That's tricky," said Cricket, "Trudi was the only one who couldn't have slashed and waxed, she was with Della and me.

As for taking the will, it could have been any of them, except Hazel, I guess."

"Not so fast," Foster piped up, "We can't assume that the others didn't have alibis, just because they weren't in our sight. The sheriff can verify that. As for breaking into the law-yer's office, that takes skill, or opportunity."

"I need to find out who has been to see him," Della said, "that could shed some light on this situation."

We also discussed the fact that if we could find out who has been snooping around the estate, it could be the thief. Con-sidering the events of the last few days, we thought it best to light a fire under our long-johns. We needed to be resourceful if we wanted answers. We had a boot print to track down and a will to search for. Foster needed to get the hidden sensor cam-eras in place. There were tapes to listen to and paperwork to sift through. The lawyer needed to be contacted, as well as Bartison's office.

"If someone wanted us to quit after being threatened," Cricket said, "They haven't lived in the far north before. The deeper the snow, the more determined we get."

"Exactly," Foster said, "When the snow gets deep, the boots come on and we get shoveling."

I wrapped my arm around his shoulder and said, "We have a heap of snow to shovel through. There have been a lot of un-answered questions and odd occurrences since those dark clouds came to town. I want to know why Trudi was on the Red Earth Road."

"I'd like to know why my dogs scented that lost sister over there, too," Peter said.

"I'd like to know more about the people in the pictures," Cricket said looking at me, "and what went on at those par-ties."

"I need to make a list of my questions," said Foster, "along with some answers, I hope."

We turned toward Della. She took her last sip of coffee, stared into the cup and said softly, "I'd like to know what my father is trying to tell me."

♦♦ 16 ♦♦

Snow, snow, snow, snow, snow!...
While we had been snuggled up inside Cricket's cozy home, about three inches of snow had fallen. The world outside sparkled. It was a soft, almost surreal, snowscape. It was quiet. There wasn't a moving vehicle in sight. Flakes floated through the glow of the streetlamps, landing in puffy mounds on wooden benches, storefront sills and sign posts. There wasn't even a breeze, which again, was extremely unusual for our little Superior town. The only footprints desecrating the blanket of pure white were the ones we had made in front of Superior Sweets. After we said our evening farewells, I stood for a while watching as the snowfall became heavier. It was filling in the tire tracks of my friend's vehicles. Within minutes my hat was coated in white. With a brush and a shake I shed some of the excess and climbed into my Explorer.

By the time I reached my lakeside cottage the snow was blowing in icy wisps across the road. In a matter of minutes the serene Christmas village setting had changed. The temperature had raised a notch mixing the snow with ice. Shards pricked my checks as I made my way to the door. It would have been beautiful, my cabin tucked in among the snow covered pines, if I could have opened my eyes wide enough to look at it.

Inside the cats were curled on fleecy blankets. I thought about lighting a fire, but instead opted for the warm goosedown quilt of my bed.

The wind was gaining momentum as I lay in the dark listening to it crack tree branches and toss snow against the roof. Needles of ice stabbed at the windows creating an unnerving staccato. Glass rattled; boughs moaned. The cats would flinch and I cowered under the covers.

I jumped when the phone rang. It was Foster checking to see if I made it home safe. He offered to come over. I let him know that I was fine; nestled in bed with the Pixie and Pan. After we hung up I was warmed by my friend's concern. The feeling passed as a rumbling coursed down the roof and splintered along the window frame. Just snow and wind, I told the cats. More hissing snow slapped the panes, whistled down the chimney and clattered across the shingles. Eventually, each of the eerie storm sounds became familiar repetitions rather than threatening audio assaults from the dark. My eye lids grew heavy and I fell into a nervous sleep. I was wrenched awake by a ghastly howl that pierced the rhythmic fury. I laid and waited. Then after falling back asleep another wicked blast would bring my eyes open with a jolt. I must have finally succumbed to accepting the onslaught and slept for a few short hours. I awoke shivering. The wind felt as if it had seeped though every wood crevasse it could find.

Finally, I got up and surrendered to the December storm. It won. I was not going to be able to sleep. Every gnashing in the iced night matched the thoughts wielding through my mind. I decided to get out Nana's *Sorting Stones*.

They were like petrified snowballs in my hand; small white and cold. As I rolled them round and round in my palm, they warmed from the friction. Focused on the stones rather than my fragmented thoughts I began plopping each of the smooth rocks onto my quilt. Some fell into the blanket's folds. Others rolled into dips in the soft material. The last one I held onto. I looked for each of them while counting: one and two were in plain sight. Stones three, four and five were peeking from under the fabric creases. Stone six was in my hand and number seven I had to search for. It was hidden.

What I held in my hand was that which both Della and I held dear; *True North*, and its lands. Out in the open were the facts; the will was missing and the property had a proposed buyer.

Half hidden were the motives for stealing the will, searching for the copy of the documents and trying to endanger those of us determined to protect the estate. The final stone suggested something hidden; possibly a secret that is not yet apparent or a motive still to be revealed. I searched for the last of the *Sorting Stones*. It wasn't until I shook the coverlet that it fell to the floor, bounced and rolled under the bed. Climbing down on hands and knees I reached for it. My fingers moved back and forth over the thinning carpet. As I touched it a bitter quiver ran through me. I bent my head back to stretch my arm even further under the low bed. I could barely grasp the elusive stone. As I did, my reflex was to let it go, leave it be. I had to make a choice. I tightened my grip, pulled the stone from its shadowy shelter and stared at it. It was small in my hand but, represented the relevant information that held the truth to this entire situation. What was it that was escaping us? How could I find what was hidden?

An ice coated tree branch scraped across the window making the sound of glass etching glass. It grated in my ears. I wanted it to stop. I finally had to move to another room. Maybe to find out this secret I'd have to get away from the negativity and confusion. Find my answers somewhere else. Obviously the cousins weren't going to talk. I curled up on the couch and fell asleep.

* * *

The morning sun was dull as it eased through the frosted window panes. An icy film fogged the air. The storm had passed, leaving in its wake a taunting north wind. Out the window, Lake Superior lay cold and frozen; completely unchanged by the evening's barrage.

After a quick inspection of my home, to make sure nothing was pilfered by the storm, I headed to town. Over the course of the night, nearly two feet of heavy snow had landed on Ottawa. School was cancelled, so youngsters were manned with shovels to earn extra Christmas cash. Snowblowers hummed behind sprays of white dust. Plows scraped as close to pavement as possible, clearing travel routes on the roads. Trucks barreled through drifts and cars pressed their transmissions while rocking back and forth to break free from snow mounds.

Two bundled ten year olds were shoveling a path in front of the café when I arrived. They were whispering about the crazy lady across the street. I looked toward the Dancing Spirit Gift Shop. There was Hazel throwing snowballs at cars. After planting icy orbs on their windshields, which made them swerve, she'd yell after them about being bad drivers. So much for thinking she was always good-hearted. I crossed the street while shaking my head. After a cheery hello, she agreed to join me for breakfast.

Peter and Judd were already seated when we jingled into the Shipwreck Café. Hazel sniffed the air, looked around and headed for another table. I grabbed her arm and aimed her back to where the sheriff sat. She continued to sniff, but followed. Before we could even order coffee the door opened with such force that it nearly jingled the bell onto the floor. Priscilla Farmington threw her hands in the air, then over her chest. Through short heaving breathes she exclaimed, "The roof…has fallen in…on the…community center."

Judd and Peter pushed back their chairs in unison and went to her. After a moment of conversation, which I could not hear over Hazel's chattering and sniffing, they returned for their jackets. Before I could speak with Priscilla the three of them jangled out the door. I looked at Hazel and decided to wait for Della.

This alone time with the crazy cousin would be a good opportunity to ask a few questions, "Hazel, who was the old lady you were talking to the other day at the motel?" She looked at me blankly.

I tried another, "Do you like it in Ottawa?" She nodded and continued folding her napkin into a bird of sorts.

"Is your room at the motel nice?" She held up the paper creation and said, "I like crafts. Blair says I'm good at them."

I tried a different approach, "I think you saw a woman looking at you through your motel window."

She raised the napkin by its wings and said, "This is for you."

My questions were futile. Before we had finished a half cup of coffee, Foster blew through the door. Reaching the table, he began excitedly, "I couldn't sleep last night and thankfully the power didn't go out. I searched the Internet and found out..." He stopped and looked at Hazel. Whispering in my ear, he gestured to my breakfast guest and said, "I better wait to tell you."

"I don't think it matters," I said.

Della, followed by Blair, blustered in the door. The tidy cousin looked disheveled. Her hair was sticking out as if she woke up, threw on her jacket, and didn't give it a look or a comb. Blair's sweat pants mopped the floor as she sprinted toward our table. Planting her hands firmly on the table top she said directly to Hazel, "What have I told you about leaving; and not telling me. I was worried sick."

Hazel looked at her and said, "Lexi and I are having breakfast. There were these boys outside throwing snowballs at cars. Are you going to have pancakes?"

Blair plopped into a chair. Raking her hands through her hair she must have finally realized that she hadn't tended to herself that morning. She said, "No Hazel, we're going home. Actually I wish we were going home, instead were going back to the motel."

She stood up and handed her sister her coat. Turning toward Della she said, "I had planned on leaving today, but the roads are bad; maybe tomorrow." Hazel waved as they left the café.

Foster scooted in close to Della and me, "I have news. I searched more about Bartison. I found a chat room where a group of people were talking about property in a little town along Lake Superior." He stopped for a minute to sip his coffee.

Della nudged him on, "Was that all?"

He shook his head. "It seems that they have big plans to buy this property and turn it into their own private hot spot, not a community resort," Foster said proudly.

"How do you know they're talking about *True North*?" I asked.

"I kept searching message boards and chat rooms, until I found where they were talking with other people over the last month," he said while looking perplexed. I guessed it was spurned from an uncertainty about how technical to get with us about surfing the web.

"Okay," I said, "What did they say?"

"It seems that they heard about this perfect property through a friend who lives in the same town in Wisconsin as Trudi and Beth Ann. They mentioned the estate, and the cabins. They talked about the owner dying and it being left to six women in one family," he paused, "Finally, I found a place where they mentioned Ottawa, Bartison and their secluded secret acquisition all in the same entry."

He looked at us and said, "It has to be it."

Della sat back in her chair, "I wonder if Trudi and Beth Ann know this?"

"Either way," I said, "I'm sure Bartison does. He has been lying the whole time, maybe even to your cousins."

"What should we do?" Foster asked.

I told them that there was a town meeting planned for tonight. They would probably be discussing Holly Fest because of the disaster at the community center. I had also heard that Bartison was going to present his plan to the city council. Foster thought we should keep our information quite, so that we'd catch him off guard.

"We don't want him to have time to prepare a rebuttal," Foster said in a mock professional tone using his index finger to push his glasses up on his nose.

"Exactly," I said tapping the table, "We do need to tell Cricket, Peter and Judd so they can be ready in case the cousins go postal."

Della smiled for what seemed to be the first time in days, "How delightful it will be, to see Trudi squirming in her designer panties." We agreed.

♦♦ 17 ♦♦

I'm gettin' nuttin' for Christmas, 'cause I ain't been nuttin' but bad...

Passing along information and shoveling walkways took up most of Della's and my day. The meeting was planned for six o'clock that evening. It had to be relocated due to the collapsed roof at the community building. Lyda offered the Northern Lights Restaurant. That's where we congregated.

A nervous excitement was bubbling in my stomach. Della would switch back and forth from fidgeting with her silverware to sitting yoga-still with her hands resting gracefully in her lap. We had helped Lyda set a head table for the council by the fireplace; the hot seat she had whispered to me. I think the mendacious real estate broker, William Bartison, was the more likely candidate for the hot seat tonight.

Peter and Judd arrived with a cluster of other town folk. Priscilla Farmington nudged her way through the crowd, scampering to the front table. Bob McMahon, the Chamber of Commerce Director, was also on the town council. He took a seat next to the museum director cum Holly Fest coordinator. Frank LaRonn, as the council chairman, pulled a chair to the center of the table. He was well respected in Ottawa as the oldest of the three brothers and two sisters who made up the prospering business conglomerate, Voyageur Enterprises. The family was always well represented at the town meetings. The LaRonns held a great deal of influence in Ottawa. They had a number of businesses between them and their spouses. Each of the enterprises began with the company trademark name Voyageur; hailed for their French-Canadian heritage.

Councilwoman, Faye Erickson was not yet present. She and her husband Leif owned Superior Realty and Superior Rustic. Faye sold the properties and Leif furnished them. She was not only an educated woman in her late thirties; she also held Ottawa's growth and prosperity in high regard. The more the town flourished so did their businesses. That was how most of the council members felt. Except for Thorndike Hendershot; Thorny, as he was referred to by most of the town, had a different idea. At seventy-two, he wanted to keep Ottawa safe from being citified. He created good checks-and-balances within the board by keeping the spirit of the town as his priority when many were influenced by financial interests. Thorny always sat at the far left. I believe, that way he could hear from his good ear; the right.

Faye, along with the last two board members arrived. Regina Walker, postmistress, and Herb Norberg, our captain-cook at the Shipwreck Café, took their seats.

During all the shuffling through of people, Foster and Cricket had joined us. Foster began to tell how he'd uncovered some amazing information when he glanced at the door. William Bartison had arrived with Trudi, Beth Ann, Blair and Hazel. Della tapped my shoulder and pointed discreetly toward the back wall. There stood her sister, Moira. She was skulking in the shadows, at least I thought so. Dressed in her head-to-toe black attire she could have been a shadow. After Bartison and escorts had passed, Foster said, "I found out some more..."

Before he could finish, Frank tapped the gavel to the table and called the meeting to order. There were at least fifty people sitting around wooden dining tables sipping refreshments and nibbling on small cakes and other finger foods Lyda had provided. The cousins sat with William Bartison at a table near the front of the room. We were sitting near the middle.

"First order of business," Frank began, "pertains to the damage done to the Community Center."

He turned the meeting over to Priscilla. She rose and began to speak, "As some of you may know the center's back roof collapsed today from the heavy snow and ice. Voyageur Construction is working on repairs, but it will not be completed in time for Holly Fest. This has me, and the rest of the committee, very upset. We don't know where to hold the festival, or if we should postpone it?"

The crowd began to buzz, each table huddled into conversation. Frank tapped his gavel once. The room quieted as if a mute button had been pushed above their heads. Priscilla cleared her throat and asked, "Does anyone have any ideas?"

Roy Jarvis, an older native of the town and co-owner of Ottawa Outfitters, stood up in his wool pants, suspenders and

Stormy Kromer hat framing his reddened cheeks, and said, "We could just have it outdoors; in the Two Feathers Park, by the store."

Old Thorny nodded while Priscilla nervously scanned the crowd for other options. Lyda offered the Northern Lights, but shyly said it probably wasn't large enough. Priscilla thanked her and sadly agreed.

It was a surprise to me when Della stood and said, "If you'd like…I mean if you thought it would work for your fest…it could be held at *True North*." She quickly sat down. Her cheeks were flushed.

She looked at me and whispered, "What do you think?" I looked from her to Priscilla.

I smiled at my friend, stood and said, "As a member of the Holly Fest committee, I think that the True estate would be a wonderful place to hold the event." I paused. The room was too quiet. I continued; actually I think I began to ramble, "It's heated. Peter's been over there working and has been getting everything fixed, even the plumbing. I know it's not the Community Center, but it is beautiful."

No one came to my rescue, so I went on, "There used to be parties there. It's big enough. The kitchen works. It would be fun to decorate."

Della whispered, "Its okay Lexi, maybe they don't want to have it there."

Mabel Norberg, who was sitting at the next table stood up and said, "Nonsense, it would be perfect. Don't you agree Priscilla? And besides, I'd love to see the old place again. It's been a lot of years since us old timers have been there. It was beautiful; remember Thorny?"

He nodded. Priscilla nodded. Bob McMahon made a motion to hold Holly Fest at *True North*. Before a second could be made, Trudi stood, stomped her foot and said, "Now just hold on."

She looked right at Della and said, "Don't you think we should have talked this over. Why do you think you can make this decision on your own?"

I though Della should have leaped across the room and choked her for making a public spectacle of their family's disagreeableness. Instead, she stood up and said, "Well dear cousin, I thought, that with the proposal you'll be making this evening, that you had the town's best interest at heart. And this is an excellent way for our property to serve the people of Ottawa."

Trudi ran her hand down the length of her brightly striped scarf and grudgingly said, "I guess it would a good thing." She sat down and took a long drink of her Appletini. Bartison patted her wrist.

Faye Erickson cut into the tension by seconding Bob's motion. Frank asked for all in favor, and the ayes had it. It was unanimous. One of the younger members of the group said that they'd never been there, and asked what it was like. Mabel winked at Della and told the crowd that the lodge was beautiful. She explained a little about the interior and assured everyone that it was a more than ample mansion-like place for Holly Fest.

Peter leaned close to Della and said, "I think we're going to be busy the next few days."

She smiled back at him, laid a slender hand on his wool jacket and said, "Thank you Peter, you're a beacon in my night."

Priscilla motioned me over and began asking a hundred questions. Frank interrupted politely. I told Priscilla not to worry; it would be just fine and that I'd talk with her in the morning. She settled back in her chair.

Frank tapped his gavel once again and the room stilled. "We have another piece of business concerning the True estate tonight," he said. He introduced William Bartison as a real estate broker from Minneapolis.

Squaring his shoulders and buttoning his suit coat, Bartison walked to the front of the room. His appearance was impressive. I felt anxious. I looked at Foster and he shook his head while holding up a finger as a gesture to wait for a minute.

William Bartison was an excellent speaker. He laid out an enticing plan for the estate properties complete with community pool facilities, convention hall and mini-golf. He leaned heavily on the tourist revenue angle. He spiced up the presentation with perks for the residents of Ottawa, such as free use of the pool and golf course.

As I looked around, I saw dollar signs in everyone's eyes. The atmosphere in the room swam with positive approval. I was jolted back to his speech as his baritone voice said, "I'd like the support of the council and the people of this fine town, on this endeavor."

The council members began conversing quietly with each other. I looked at Foster. He mouthed, just be patient.

Finally, Frank said, "We'll open the meeting up for discussion."

Foster waited a polite moment. When no one else spoke up, and Bartison was looking extremely confident, Foster stood up. "I have few questions for our guest," he said. Trudi shot a glare at our table. It was ignored.

Foster pulled out a small notebook and asked, "Do you know a Diana Vandersmith?"

Cricket and I looked at Foster quizzically. Della, Judd and Peter were slightly more restrained even though they also realized that this wasn't what we had talked about. I surmised that maybe he'd gotten the name from his web searches. As I looked back toward the tall man in the blue suit he was visibly squirming. He didn't answer Foster.

"She knows you," Foster continued, "it seems she knows you very well." Bartison seemed to be moving away from the crowd. He was eyeing the door nervously. I was wondering what Foster was up to.

"Actually," Foster said, "she and I had a long talk today on the phone. It appears that you are not a legitimate real estate agent. It also seems that you are not being completely honest about your dealings here."

Bartison finally spoke, "You don't know what you're talking about."

"Yes I do." Foster turned to the council and continued, "We have been lied to. After purchasing *True North*, this man and a number of his wealthy friends plan to build a big fence around the property and use it as a vacation party playground. From what I understand, there will not be any public access, even along the beach. There will be no pool for our use, or mini-golf. From what I understand, there will be private parties: excessive and very private parties."

There were a few irritated gasps of *Well I never...* and *How dare he....* Then there was a loud voice saying, "That is not true. I can vouch for this man and his intentions."

It was Trudi who had stomped to his side and had spoken. She looked at Foster and said, "Whoever your source is must be wrong. Or maybe you made it up."

All eyes turned from the ranting Trudi back to Foster. Rather than answer her directly, he aimed his next remark to Bartison, "Miss Vandersmith suggests that you get your cheating tail back home right now or the engagement is off."

Foster sat down. After a momentary pause of processing the fiancé information, Trudi then squealed curses at Bartison and the crowd in general. Beth Ann came to her side to support her nearly fainting figure. I glanced at Moira she was chuckling behind a black gloved hand.

Bartison nearly ran from the room, and probably high tailed it out of town, as his fiancé suggested. Foster filled us in after Frank adjourned the meeting. After his searches didn't produced anything more, he went back to the engagement announcement posted in the Minneapolis newspaper. He called Diana Vandersmith and explained that her fiancé was in Ottawa posing as the boyfriend of a land owner. A woman's wrath, he explained with a smile, opens the door for a great source of information.

Foster concluded, "After she cleared up the details, I checked on her. She's extremely wealthy."

"It's ironic," Cricket said, "how Trudi was after Bartison for his money, and he appears to be after this other woman for hers. They may have both screwed themselves over."

"At least they didn't screw over Ottawa," Foster said.

"Thanks to you," Della hugged him.

Moira ambled over to our table. She looked at Foster, "Nice work, kid. Keep that up and you might have a big truck like me some day." She laughed and went over to talk to Thorny.

Cricket clapped her hands together and said, "One bad guy down. Still, one bad girl to go."

"The will," Della said.

I wrapped my arm around Della, "We'll keep working on that. But, for now, it looks like we have a party to plan."

Foster's uncle, Bob McMahon joined us along with Frank LaRonn, Herb and Mabel. Bob congratulated his nephew as Frank added, "You saved us a lot of trouble by uncovering that scoundrel. I've always felt you were a good journalist."

Mabel was talking with Della about *True North*. She was very excited to see the place again and offered her help with the arrangements.

As they left, Blair and Hazel made their way to us, "Well cousin, you made quite an impression this evening. Hazel and I will be staying around for the gala. We too would like to share in the True family recognition. You aren't the only True woman here."

♦♦ 18 ♦♦

Don't you tell a single soul what I'm going to say…
Della B. True, Moira B. True, Blair B. True, Hazel B. True, Beth Ann B. True and Trudi B. True made me wonder which of them were actually true. Della was exhausted and retired to the Belle Star. Foster, Cricket and I escaped to my cabin. We had some sorting to do.

Now that Bartison was out of the picture we could concentrate on finding the copy of the will. Della had told us that her father's safety deposit box had been emptied and the will was not among the items recovered. She had said there wasn't any paperwork kept at the bank only a few pieces of heirloom jewelry that had been her mother's. Obviously, her dad had kept his important possessions someplace else.

Cricket played out possibilities, "Women, like my grandma, often keep their treasures in a girdle box, coat pockets or tucked away in a drawer. Men on the other hand feel that the freezer or the mattress is better than a bank. My grandpa buried cans of coins in the yard. My dad stashes things in the rafters."

"Della's dad was a business man," Foster added, "Maybe he had a home safe?"

"It would have to be at *True North*, their family home was sold years ago," I said.

"We need to look harder," Cricket was poised for attack, as determined as if there was a brood of bears between her and a plate of cinnamon buns; and she'd win.

It was unanimous that we hadn't actually done a thorough search of the lodge. We hadn't checked rafters or freezers. Possibly even the mattresses would offer a lead.

"I'll be there with Della tomorrow cleaning and putting up decorations," I said, "If you can get some help at the shop maybe you can stop by."

Cricket nodded, and then turned to Foster, "Did you ever get those cameras in place?"

"Maybe tomorrow we can hide them behind the holly," he looked over the top of his glasses, "I forgot, sorry."

"Hey, you did a lot," I told him, "above and beyond; don't feel bad. We all feel like we should be doing more. I was supposed to call Bartison's office and never did it. I have been watching boot tracks, when I remember, but none have been a match to those we saw by the estate."

"Speaking of duty," Cricket said, "Judd sure has been quiet lately."

I filled her in, "When we stopped to see him about Bartison, he told Della how peeved he was at her family. They had each other and were acting horribly. He said that he missed his family."

"Are they coming for Holly Fest?" Cricket asked.

"He wasn't sure, but probably not."

We sipped hot chocolate and stared into the fire. The cats were purring on laps and Christmas music was softly filling the cabin with warm memories. My family would be here for the weekend, Cricket's lived in town and Foster had said his mom was planning on coming for the holidays, but probably not for the festival. Della most likely called her daughter as soon as she reached the Inn. The rest of the True clan didn't have family. They were all they had. There were a lot of people who didn't have anyone to share the holidays with. As cheery as Christmas was for some, it was also a reminder to others of their seclusion. I wondered about Thorny, Joe Hill and the old woman I'd seen, and about the rock shop guy and

Regina Walker. Did they have family? Some of them created extended families with friends in Ottawa, but some people had no one. I wondered who Moira had spent her Christmastimes with.

The excitement of foiling Bartison's plans dwindled as did the night. Cricket and Foster donned their winter garb and headed for home. I sat with my little family, Pixie and Pan, until the fire died down and the music chimed its last note. As I curled under the comforter the phone rang. The voice on the other end of the line was muffled and angry, "Leave it alone. Leave them alone. Keep your nose out of our business. You think you're so smart. Well, you're not. Some things are better off left to lie with the dead. You're ruining everything. Do you understand?"

"Who is this?" The line went dead. I lay in the dark thinking. It was hard to tell who was speaking. I wasn't even sure if it was a man or a woman. I repeated the conversation over and over. *Leave them alone* is what was said, not leave us alone. *Our business...*who else would consider the True Estate as part of their business? *Some things are better off left to lie with the dead...*That sounded like a secret to me. It was nearly midnight. I'd wait until morning to talk with Della. Maybe she knew of a secret worth threatening someone for, to keep it hidden.

♦♦ 19 ♦♦

And every mother's child is going to spy...

"I think I may have found out why the will and other documents were stolen," I said to Della as I sat on her bed in her newly appointed room, the *Daniel Moore*. Fish and moose wallpaper encircled the tiny room. Handcrafted willow chairs were propped by a small pine table. As I sat on one of them, eyeing a bronze sculpture of a black bear, I explained my late night phone call.

"So my family has some long hidden secret?"

"That would be my guess. Any idea what it might be?"

She paced the length of the dark green carpeting. Her arms, covered in a plaid Pendleton wool jacket, crossed and uncrossed. The only sound in the room was the material of her slate gray slacks swooshing in rhythm with her gait. Finally, she stopped and sat next to me on at the table, "Years ago, I had a very bad experience at the lodge."

She looked down at her hands. "I've never talked to anyone about it. So, I can't imagine that would be it." I waited. Silence has a way of keeping the other person speaking; and she did.

"When I was a teenager, Thorny and his younger brother Marcus would do odd jobs for my dad. Marcus was older than me; I was sixteen and he was about twenty. Moira thought he was dreamy, but he had eyes for me. One evening, on the beach, he took me off into the bushes. I was young and scared. He acted sweet, but he wasn't and he raped me. I never told anyone."

I began to console her. She brushed it off, "Oh don't worry, it was a long time ago. I've put it past me. It was a little hard going into the lodge that first night. You see, after it happened I locked myself in my room, with that raggedy doll, and cried. I never wanted to be in the lodge ever again. Until the other night, I hadn't."

"What happened to Marcus?"

"I heard that he died of cancer in his late forties. Thorny had taken care of him, and Moira had kept in touch with the old guy over the years. She was so jealous of Marcus that she swooned over Thorny. Being the older brother, he was smarter than to return the affections of a teenager."

"Do you think Marcus told anyone?"

"I don't know. I rather doubt it. If my father would have found out he would have killed him."

I looked at her. Her eyes were drained and tired. "Maybe that has nothing to do with this. There would not be anything about that summer in the will. So, that still doesn't explain why it's missing."

She agreed as she pulled on her coat, "Let's go over to the estate and concentrate on getting things spruced up for Holly Fest. I want to bring the place back to life. My dad would like that"

Peter was already busy working on fussy light fixtures, loose flooring and sticky doors when we arrived. Della's disposition perked up when she saw him, "Good morning Mr. Holloway. You've been here so often that you must be getting behind on your other work. I'm sorry for taking up all your precious time."

"It's winter," he said coming down off a ladder, "There isn't a lot of work. Besides, even if there was I'd make you my priority."

Feeling the warmth rising through the dust, I snuck off to the kitchen in search of cleaning supplies. We spent all morning polishing woodwork, shining marble, airing upholstery and bedding, along with scouring sinks, toilets and tiles. Cricket joined in around mid-morning bringing with her a collection of nostalgic Christmas music. Bing Crosby and Nat King Cole swooned our spirits as we glossed the gilt and buffed the brass. Peter captured cobwebs from the higher reaches while Cricket wrestled dust bunnies from under furnishings. Foster arrived at lunchtime with vegetable soup and corned beef sandwiches from the Lumberjack Kitchen. We ate like bears in spring.

After devouring every last crumb, even ones too small for a mouse, Della poured coffee, to go with the jelly thumbprint cookies Cricket had made earlier in the morning. Foster pulled papers from a folder and showed them to Della, "Here is a list of Blair's clients. I thought you might want to take a look at it." While she was scanning the names, he produced another print out.

"This is a list of the legal documents your dad had registered over the past ten years," he said laying it on the table. "I looked it over and noticed a number of quick claim deeds."

Peter looked at the paperwork, "These kinds of transfers only happen with the sale of property."

"My dad had the business that sold. There were also some warehouses and then his home. Maybe that's what they're from."

"It's hard to say," Foster was looking over the listings, "there are only registration dates; not lengthy descriptions."

Della had been focusing on Blair's client list. She looked up from the sheet of names for only a moment to discuss the property transfers with Foster. She pushed both pages toward Foster and said, "It's possible that there are answers to our questions somewhere within all this information, I just can't seem to sort it out. I just wish we'd find dad's will. It would be so much easier."

She busily began cleaning up cups and plates, "It irritates me that the lawyer let the documents be stolen." The cups teetered and one fell to floor and smashed.

Tears filled her eyes, "I just don't know what to do? This should be a time when family pulls together. Instead, it's a mess; just like that," she pointed to the broken glass. Cricket and I began picking up the pieces while reassuring her that everything would be alright.

"We'll figure it out," I said.

Foster took Della back to the Inn to rest. Peter went home. As Cricket and I sat alone in the stillness of the big house she got a sparkle in her eye. Scanning the space around us, she said, "Let's search."

Discarding our cleaning cloths, we rubbed our palms together and began in the kitchen. We clattered through every cupboard, tapped on every inch of wallboard and did a tap dance across the floor. We found nothing hidden, hollow or loose. In the dining room we repeated the ritual. Again our hopes were dashed.

The great room took considerably more time. There were extensively more wall and floor spaces. Each piece of furniture was patted down. Every carpet inspected for trap doors. We opted to leave the den until last, seeing we'd searched it before. After a quick snack of cookies and strong coffee we began climbing to the second floor.

About half way up Cricket turned sharply and said, "We should really check the hallway and stairs first." Even though the entrance was large, it was also sparsely furnished. There was a coat rack, a beautifully upholstered chair, an area rug over the tiled floor and two small cherrywood tables. Cricket moved each object and scanned the vicinity with felonious precision.

"You look like a pro," I told her while performing a hand-to-wood massage over each stair step, with my special gloves snugged over my skin.

"Years of practice," she answered while opening the closet door, "Between cheating boyfriends and the cats, I've become an expert at ferreting out hidden items." I could hear her clanking coat hangers, upending shoes and rearranging boxes.

"Nothing here," she announced reappearing from the under the stairs' hideaway. We took deep breaths and mounted the steps. I started with the master bedroom; she began at the far end of the hall with one of the smaller guest rooms.

"You never know," she said, "Sometimes the best place to hide something is right under someone's nose."

I began the search under the bed. It was one place I hadn't looked before. There were two storage boxes tucked neatly beneath the old bedsprings. Laying flat on my stomach, I reached under and pulled them out. A sense of hope began to quicken my heart beat. I opened the first. It held blankets. Disappointment allowed me to uncover the second box without much anticipated excitement. As I lifted the lid I regained my optimism. It held a variety of personal item; hairbrushes, jewelry boxes, perfume bottles, beaded purses and silky scarves. I decided to take off one of my thin skin-like gloves. Using my other hand I gently moved the items around. I spotted a small light blue woman's handkerchief bunched inside an envelope. I lifted it out and held it in my uncovered hand.

Everything was dark. I was crying in heavy sobs with the small piece of cotton held over my eyes. As I bunched it into my hand, I placed it against my breast. My eyes were closed. The sobs were slowing to gasps of breath. I opened my eyes to the bedroom's dim light. I could hear the waves outside. Reaching for an object on my lap, I held up a framed photo and again began to sob as I stared at the image of a man and woman. The man was Norville True. The woman wore a polka dot dress.

I could hear Cricket calling my name. I laid the delicate blue fabric back into the box and went to her. "Help me move this," she said, and then looked at my face, "Have you been crying?"

I rubbed at my cheeks. There were tears on them. I told her about the vision. She hurried me back to the master bedroom and the box of 1940's treasures. She clawed through them, trying on scarves and spraying perfume; a kid in a costume closet.

After a few more squirts of perfume, she stopped and looked at me in horror, "Maybe I shouldn't have touched anything. Oh Lexi, I'm sorry. I got so excited."

I assured her it was alright. The only thing that appeared out of place was the blue handkerchief. As she rummaged through the box she agreed. It was the only blue item. The rest of the contents were splashed in cheery lemons, corals and rosy pinks. I pulled my little glove back on as we went to move a large cedar chest filled with blankets. There wasn't anything under it, so we moved it back.

All during the remainder of the upstairs' search my mind kept wandering back to the framed photo. It was familiar, but I was sure that it had not been in with the photo albums Della had shown us. Where had I seen it? The inability to remember gnawed at me. Still, we continued trying to outwit Carsen True in his own house. So far, he was winning and we were losing.

"One room left," Cricket said, "the den."

"Don't forget the basement." I shivered.

♦♦ 20 ♦♦

Have a cup of cheer...

Cricket's aversion to mice and mine to spiders made our search of the basement short-lived. Cobwebs loomed in dense curtains over places that may have held secret passageways. They would have to stay forever hidden unless Foster cared to brave the tangled webs. Mouse droppings caked the rafters. It was more than either of us could force ourselves to endure. It was starting to get dark outside, bringing up images of frothing rats and tortoise-sized tarantulas.

Above us, creaking floorboards moved us hurriedly up the repaired wooden stairs.

Blair and Hazel met us in the great room. Cricket gave me a look, as if saying *We won't be searching the den today.*

"We saw your vehicle and thought we'd see if you needed any help," Blair said while scanning the newly polished room.

Even in the low light of dusk the room glimmered of assidu-
ousness. The hours we had spent manicuring the estate was
evident.

We informed her that we were meeting Della for dinner
and hadn't planned on decorating until the next day. She didn't
offer to help. I think she was just being nosy. Hazel was walking from window to window peering out at the snowscape, "I
remember playing under those pine trees."

She tilted her head in thought and then walked past us until
she reached the arched doorway leading to the entrance hall.
She looked up the flight of stairs and said, "I remember playing in the attic, too."

As soon as she said it, *the attic,* it jogged my memory. I
grabbed Cricket's arm and said, "We have to go. Maybe we'll
see you tomorrow." I rushed her past Hazel. While fastening
my last coat button, I was stuffing Cricket into her jacket and
shoving her out the door.

"What are you doing?" she insisted. I hushed her and
hopped into the Explorer. As she got into the passenger side it
dawned on me that her little beater car was nowhere in sight.
"My dad dropped me off earlier," she said as if reading my
mind, "Now tell me what that was about."

"We have to get over by Foster before he closes up at the
newspaper. I need to see his pictures of the attic."

We arrived at the brick front building of Northbound
Books and the Ottawa Ledger. Macy Buckland, who was filling in while the receptionist was on maternity leave, was getting ready to lock the door. She told us that Foster had gone up
to Mission Point to do a story and wouldn't be back until later.
After we chatted about Holly Fest along with her excitement
about *True North* we said good night.

"I'll have to wait," I said feeling disheartened. Cricket reminded me that we had to pick up Della for supper. So we
headed back through town. Evening had settled quickly and
the twinkling lights starred the street. Christmastime in Ottawa

looked magical. I turned on the radio and found a station playing carols. We sang our way to the Lighthouse Inn.

Della looked rested in a navy fleece jacket worn over the top of a turtleneck sporting crystal blue snowflakes. She even had on one of her signature hats; a winter-white cashmere boater with a soft brim and rounded cap. "You look much better," I told her.

"I feel better," she said and pulled on a nicely tailored sheepskin coat and matching boots, "Where are we eating?"

"I thought we'd stop at the Pirate's Cove. It's dark enough in there no one will notice if Cricket and I are wearing cobwebs."

She laughed and assured us we looked fine, and that it would be nice to visit with Kat, also. When we arrived at the cozy saloon it was decorated in Christmas golds and royal blues. Coins dangled from garlands made of jewels. The festiveness had escaped me the last time we were there. Kat was off for the evening and her brother Forrest was manning the ship. Not long after ordering our food, two peevish cousins pirated into the cove.

It was obvious that they had already been into the whiskey kegs; or whatever their mash of choice was. With a stumble and a bump they aimed for the bar. Trudi swiveled precariously on her stool. Spotting us, she slid from her perch and stalked to our table with words lashing, "I can not believe you did that. Yes I can. You have always wanted it all for yourself." Beth Ann maneuvered to her side as she continued, "Are you happy now that you made a fool of me. I need that money. But, don't worry dear cousin; I've got a backup plan." Beth Ann grabbed her arm, whispering for her to be quite. Trudi pulled away, "You just wait and see. You'll wish you'd left things alone. I'm no one to mess with."

With that she went to the bar, tossed down her drink, threw her chin in the air and zigzagged out the door with Beth Ann following in the wake of hot pink wrath.

"Well," Cricket said, "that was pleasant. At least she wasn't packing a gun."

Della displayed the expressions of sad, embarrassed and angry all at the same time.

I tried to ease her concern, "She took a hard blow yesterday. Lashing out is to be expected while licking her wound."

Della agreed, "I feel bad for her."

"She's made her own choices," Cricket said, "It's one of those facts of life."

A loud crashing of glass erupted into our conversation. Della stared at a gaping hole in the front window pane. Cricket had jumped, nearly toppling our wooden pedestal table. I ran for the front door to see who had hurled something into the Cove. There was no one in the parking lot; no car lights leaving it.

♦♦ 21 ♦♦

Here we are as in olden days...

In the morning, a dusting of nighttime snow hid the dissonance from the previous evening. It seemed to restore the Christmas bliss back into the world. The sun was rising as it should. Chickadees were dancing from tree to feeder. A rabbit waited for fallen sunflower seeds. It was so serene. Comforting melodies of goodwill hummed through my mind.

I picked up my Nana's agate heart necklace from the end table. I began to rub it between my thumb and fingers remembering her poem: *Rub it once for luck, twice for love, and over and over for worries to fade making room for wishes to come true.* I wished that I could hold on to this magical yuletide feeling. I wished that my picture perfect scene would last.

I knew that wishes travel in threes. My euphoria was keeping me from asking for the obvious. It was difficult to acknowledge all the unrest lying just beyond my fence. I wanted to hide out in my rosy white world and pretend none of the bad things were happening. I imagined Della felt the same way. So, I wished for her; that she'd find the answers she was looking for to put her heart at rest.

As the sun rose higher, the snow came to life. It glimmered of dancing jewels jigging across the land. It was nature's *bling* at its finest. My mood became merrier. A cup of coffee for extra insurance and I was ready to deck the halls for Holly Fest.

Priscilla was to meet me at *True North,* but first I had to gather up Foster who would be my box hauler. Stored at the community center were a dozen cartons of decorations waiting for their once a year debut. Our decorating committee opted for the use of natural materials to accent the beauty of the lodge. Priscilla excitedly offered to bring some of the antique Christmas treasures she's been coveting for years.

In my state of holiday cheer, I nearly forgot to ask Foster to bring his laptop. Crime solving almost slipped my mind until Della called to inform me that she needed to go to the city and do some shopping. Mostly, I think she needed to escape for a while. A trip to the lawyer's office was also on her agenda. She was feeling guilty leaving me to trim the big house. I assured her that I would be fine. Her job would be to put the finishing touches on things; she was great with accessories. We laughed and I could tell she was relieved.

After carrying in the boxes of decorations, Foster diligently strung tiny white twinkle lights everywhere I told him. Peter had stopped by to check the wiring, and to warn us not to overload circuits. He left Foster a diagram. It was quite helpful.

Priscilla created a nostalgic display in the dining room using her antique candle holders, heirloom candy dishes and village figurines. All were placed above the reach of the children. A hand woven runner ran the length of the dining room table. She had placed non-collectible dishes along the expanse of the deep red material which would be filled with Holly Fest treats.

My morning consisted of stringing holly down the wooden banister and along archways. I arranged pine garlands with berries and cones onto mantles. With great precision I hung small wreaths on each of the windows. I was contemplating a papa-bear pile of bows when Cricket arrived at noon, just as Priscilla was leaving.

We toured the lodge admiringly, inspecting progress. "Where is Santa going to be sitting?" she asked, "And where is the tree going?"

I told her that I was waiting for her to help with that. She selected a spot toward the back of the great room for Santa. The Christmas tree she felt would be best centered by the lakeside windows.

While eating pasties and cookies, I looked through Foster's attic pictures. "There it is," I said, nearly choking on sprinkles, "that's the framed photo I saw."

* * *

Foster enlarged the image, "It's too frosty to get a clear picture of the people."

Cricket piped up, "We could go back into the attic and get it?" With a three-way glance we scraped back our chairs and scurried to the second floor. Foster had the ladder down before Cricket finished climbing the main steps. After maneuvering into the iced domain he took my flashlight and began crawling toward the old dresser on which we had spotted the photo. "I have it," he said and scuttled back to the opening.

In the warmth of the children's bedroom we brushed a layer of frost from the glass. There they were, Norville True and the woman in the polka-dot dress. We had to surmise it was powder-blue due to the fact the photo was in black and white.

"Who do you think she is?" Cricket asked. I shook my head, while staring at the faces of the couple.

"She looks familiar, but we'll have to wait and ask Della." We put the slightly tarnished framed treasure on the dining table by the computer. I looked at it again. Their faces were smiling, but the true expressions held sadness, or maybe it was nervousness. I couldn't be sure.

Cricket's mom had offered to watch the shop, so that she and I could trim 'til the reindeer came home.

Judd stopped by to check on progress, or so he said. He was strutting down the walkway, laughing with a man as large as he was and nearly the same sixty-two years of age. I had just opened the front door to usher Foster and Peter out to work on the outside lights and garlands when then mounted the steps.

Lexi, I brought you another worker," Judd said while patting the man firmly on the back.

"We can sure use the help," I said, as Cricket, Foster and Peter came up behind me.

"This is my cousin, Gunn, he's here for the holidays." Judd beamed.

Gunn gave a long whistle, "I've seen lots of places in my time, but this beats the brass. It's a dandy." Looking at his new acquaintances he said, "Judd told me it was nice, but it's unbelievable. You must be Lexi and Cricket. Nice to meet you." He shook our hands and then said to Peter, "I've heard about the dog guy; that you?" Peter nodded and they gave each other brisk handshakes.

Judd pointed to Foster, "This is the newspaper man I was telling you about."

"Heard you rattled a few relatives last night; good for you." He laughed. It was deep rich from the bottom of his hearty body.

Lexi spoke up, "I was just sending the guys out with boxes of lights. Want to help them?"

Gunn rubbed his work-worn, deerskin gloves together and said, "You bet."

Judd waved and said he'd be back later to inspect as he nearly jigged up the walk.

As we closed the door on the trio sorting lights and making man talk, Cricket put an arm around me and said, "Well, Judd sure changed glum to glee. Amazing what a little company can do for a person."

"I can't blame him. I'm so excited to have my family coming for the Fest."

"Is your mom bringing more of her pizzelis?"

I swatted her arm away and we laughed while rearranging furniture to make room for Santa and guests. A spot was cleared for the tree. The kitchen was readied for the festive foods being prepared by our neighbors. We turned the den into an extra sitting area. Each of the upstairs rooms was child-proofed. We chatted the entire time about the Christmas presents we'd bought, family gatherings we were planning on attending and additional Holly Fest details that needed to be done. We did not talk about hidden wills, family secrets or evil land dealers. This was Cricket's advice; we wanted the lodge to be cheery, not eerie.

After popping ribbons along the pines and stringing cranberry beads through the boughs we snuck out the side entrance to spy on the boys. We were hoping that their work didn't need to be redone with a feminine touch. To our surprise they had created an awe inspiring scene. They did as instructed by wrapping pine branches and lights along the log pillars and railings. To my amazement, they had lit up every tree and bush surrounding the front porch. Lighted beacons outlined the stone path leading to the entrance. Foster and Gunn were hanging silver snowflakes from the trees while Peter attached a final strand of lights around the lamppost. The most spectacular additions were icy sculptures of nutcracker soldiers guarding the stairs. Cricket whistled and I clapped and cheered, "This is wonderful. Where did you get the ice statues?"

"Peter made them," Foster said, "Aren't they great?"

We nodded, and as I looked closer said, "There are dogs by their feet; ice replicas of Ghost and Ruby. They're marvelous."

Peter finished his project and joined us, "When I moved here, I was captivated by the ice sculptures they do at the college in Houghton, so last year I learned how it was done by helping out. It's something I couldn't do in Kentucky. It's fun."

Cricket and I began giggling. It was so beautiful.

Gunn's cheeks were red and he had icicles trailing down his mustache, but he was smiling. "I haven't had this much fun working in years. I'm sure glad I came to see my cousin."

Cricket patted his arm; actually it was more like punch, "We're glad you came too. Judd was looking a little long in the face, missing family and all."

Gunn nodded, "I kind of figured that, because so was I."

Peter told us they had one more thing to do and it would be finished. He had to run home and get a bench and hitching post for Joe Hill to use for his horse-drawn sleigh. Foster and Gunn offered to ride along and help load. When they returned they also had a tree; a big, full balsam tree that was freshly cut. With a little encouragement, we wrestled it through doorways and positioned it at the far end of the great room in front of the windows just like Cricket had wanted. It was perfect. Later in the evening, when the branches had settled, we'd decorate it, with Della.

"Maybe some of her family would like to help," Cricket said, "we could ask?"

She was right; at least we would offer.

As if on cue, the four cousins pulled into the driveway. As they descended onto the premises I could hear snobbish remarks, which I'm sure were coming from Trudi. Her sister was shushing her. Blair ran a curious finger over the frozen man who stood sentinel by the stairs before ushering Hazel away from him. As they filed through the front door the men snuck out the back.

Blair called, "My, my where are those busy little imps?"

"In here," I called back from the adjoining room.

They stood in a cluster as they gazed around at their once-abandoned family vacation home. Finally Beth Ann said, "I've never seen it at Christmastime, it's quite nice."

That, I thought, was an understatement. The lodge was grand; a north pole dream castle complete with a nook for Old St. Nick to hear the children's dreams. Hazel broke free from her sister's grasp and began running from room to room, "Where are the presents?" she asked.

Then before anyone could reply she said, "Is there candy and cookies?" Her childlike questions continued, "Is my stocking going to hang by the fireplace? Will there be stories and eggnog? Will Santa know I'm here? Is it Christmas Eve? Why aren't there any ornaments on the tree?" Hazel had been skipping from room to room. Blair tried to catch her as the rest of us watched.

Cricket giggled and I elbowed her.

Finally Trudi said, "Oh for Pete's sake Blair, grab her and let's go. We saw it, now I want to leave." Blair snagged her enthusiastic charge around the waist and guided her toward the front door.

"Before you leave," I said hurrying after them, "I wanted to ask…. if you wanted to help… decorate the tree later… tonight." I stammered a bit and kept my distance as Trudi glowered at me. They looked back and forth to each other like a pack of nervous coyotes wondering if it was a trap.

Trudi took the lead, letting me know that she would not be any part of it. Beth Ann hesitated. Then followed her sister's directive, she shook her head slowly as she walked. The whole time her eyes had been wandering hopefully over their old summer haunt turned Christmas retreat.

Blair said, "We may be back."

The pack retreated, suspiciously eyeing the frigid guards, their solidified pets, the silvery snowflakes fluttering in the trees and even the lamppost as if wary of attack. Except for Hazel who was muttering soft cooing sounds.

"They sure can ruin a good thing," I said,

"Nothing some cookies and coffee can't cure," Cricket winked.

As we returned to the dining room I yelled. Cricket spun in the doorway framing the dining room and kitchen, "What?"

"The photograph; it's gone!"

◆◆ 22 ◆◆

Much pleasure thou can'st give me…

"Close your eyes," I told Della as we approached the driveway to *True North.* She had returned from her excursion to the city revived and excited to see the estate house. The sun had already set as I parked at the hitching post. "Keep them closed," I said while skittering around to her side of the vehicle. I opened the door, helped her out and positioned her a few feet away from the entrance path. "Okay, you can look now."

"Oh Lexi, it's beautiful." She turned and hugged me.

"Merry Christmas, Della."

She began to cry and laugh all at the same time.

"Everyone worked on it. Look at the ice sculptures." She was making happy sounds all the way down the path. As we walked up the porch stairs, Cricket opened the door. Peter and Foster were right behind her. "This is so very wonderful," Della said while hugging each of them in turn. Cricket nearly pulled her through the lodge giving her the grand tour.

We followed behind. Foster whispered to me, "I put the cameras up; one above the main fireplace, one in the den and another at the top of the stairs. I could only round up three of them."

I brought cider and sugary breads into where everyone had taken seats in the great room by the tree. Again, Della gushed over all the work we had done.

"Tonight we can decorate the tree," Cricket said stuffing cranberry nut bread into her mouth.

We each took turns telling her about our day, along with the visit from the cousins. "After they left we noticed the photograph was missing," I explained while reaching for a slice of the sugared cardamom bread.

"It doesn't surprise me," she answered while nibbling small pieces of fruitcake, "I found out something very interesting today at the lawyer's office". We all stopped chewing.

She continued, "It seems that his personal secretary's name is Tina Hathaway. It is one of the names on Blair's client list; one of the more prominent names."

Cricket choked, "You're kidding?"

She shook her head, "So, my guess is that Ms. Hathaway offered the means for Blair to procure the will."

"That's a great guess," Peter said, "but why? Did you figure that out?"

"No, but it will help to know *who* took it, right?"

"Oh definitely," he said offering her more cider, like a peace offering, for not being more enthused about her discovery. Seeing his discomfort, I took the initiative, "That's really great. Maybe she's the one with a secret?"

"How do we find that out?" Della asked. We told her about Foster's cameras.

I asked Cricket, "Have your sister, Jana, and her friends been snooping around at the Windigo?"

She nodded, but said they hadn't found out anything *good*.

Della stood, in her royal blue thigh-length velveteen sweater and said, "Let's not let this ruin our night. I'm feeling great and want to decorate the tree."

Foster grabbed the last piece of Polish povitica while springing toward the cartons of ornaments, "These ones are from the community center. This one is from Priscilla, antiques I think. The big red box is from my aunt Bette. She said you might like them."

Peter had begun stringing lights while Cricket, Della and I opened boxes. We were engrossed in Christmas glass Santas, miniature lighthouses and hand blown candy canes when we noticed Foster escorting Judd, Gunn and Whistler into the room.

Della, always the good hostess, greeted the guests while offering them cider and treats which she had requested Cricket get from the kitchen. Judd, with great enthusiasm, introduced his cousin to Della. She held both his thick, leathery hands in hers as she welcomed him to her home.

Judd strained to see all around the room, "The place looks great. You kids must have worked since sun-up." We beamed with pride.

He continued, "I came out because I have some news for you. Whistler asked if could ride along to see if Miss Marx had gotten a certain present for his niece? Hope it's alright that we stopped by?"

Della assured them that it was.

The sheriff went on, "I ran background checks on your family, after the incidences the other night, and found out something interesting. It seems that Moira True has a private investigator's license."

"What?" Della said and sat down hard in a chair.

* * *

Peter poked his head from the back side of the tree and said, "Well, that answers our question about what she does in her spare time."

We watched Della. She was thinking. Cricket said, "Remember when she first arrived and was asking if the candlesticks had disappeared, *too*. She must have known the will was missing."

Foster said, "I thought it was weird at the town meeting how she congratulated me and said *if I kept it up I could get a big truck like hers.* She must have been talking about investigating."

"She was awfully *clever* during the search for Hazel, too," I added.

"I'm just stunned," Della said, "and a bit embarrassed, that I didn't know."

Judd spoke up, "It seems that she runs a very low-keyed surveillance operation, according to a friend of mine, and that she's quite good."

"I bet they were her tape recorders," Cricket said. We agreed.

I looked at Foster, "What was on those tapes, did you ever find out?"

He shook his head, "They require a password to access the memory. I haven't figured it out yet, well actually my friend hasn't. He's better at that than I am."

The Christmas music had stopped. Cricket flipped the tape and *Oh, Christmas Tree* reminded us of our project. I told Whistler that I had his present for Macy and went to retrieve it from my Explorer. As I stood outside of the estate I imagined how merry the parties must have been here. The place had a life of its own.

As I handed him the small wrapped box with Macy's gift tucked neatly inside of it, I asked, "Whistler, do you remember the get-togethers the True families held here years ago?"

"Of course. They were a highlight of many Ottawa summers. Della's dad threw the best ones. Your dad was a good man. His brothers were a little snobby, but Carsen was always a friend and a gentleman."

Della patted his shoulder and offered more cider, which he accepted. As Whistler continued to spin tales of the True parties we positioned ornaments on the big balsam. Peter, Judd and Gunn sat and listened. Foster was designated for the higher placements.

"Everyone from town would come to their parties. Families brought their kids during the day. Della probably remembers playing with mine and Elwood Waverly's daughters, they were best friend back then. The LaRonn girls were there with their folks, as were the rest. Some of the parents have passed on, some of the kids moved away. But, there's still a bunch of us here that remember all the food and dancing. We'd play volleyball on the beach and horseshoes over by the garages." He took a sip of cider checking to see if we were listening, and we were, so he continued.

"Thorny and I would help with upkeep. I liked mowing lawn. Thorny liked fixing thing. Marcus was supposed to be helping, but he was more interested in swimming and girls back then, God rest his soul. One summer your uncle broke his leg and spent more than a month here. Your dad would check on him every week or so. Marcus spent a lot of time tending to Norville. He and Meredith Waverly, Mackenzie back then; they were an item. She would come in to clean and cook when the wait staff was away. I remember because they would invite the rest of us up in the evenings for drinks and food. Norville didn't mind. He was glad for the company he'd say. I didn't have a family yet, so I could stay out late. Once my family came I didn't do that anymore."

I asked, "I thought Meredith and Elwood were together?"

"That was later," he clarified, "she found out that Marcus was chasing around, like usual, and broke it off. Later, she and Elwood took up together. It was a small town, still is, we took turns dating the girls. I got lucky with my Missus, God rest her soul. We met, fell in love and got hitched. We had our wedding party out here. It looks different at Christmastime. The place was closed up during the winter. I remember one year the brothers came up hunting. They never had done that before. I got them all set up; kind of like a guide. They paid me real good too. Bought a new chainsaw and had extra Christmas money that year. That deer head above the fireplace came from that hunt. Your daddy shot it. It was a real trophy."

Della stopped and looked at Whistler, "That was about fifteen years ago, right?"

"Closer to twenty I think, "he said, "and the last time your uncles came up here, as far as I can remember. But, it's hard to say. I get the years mixed up. There were so many of them when you get to be my age. Your folks would stop in to see me and the family when they were in town. A couple of times they had us out for a Sunday picnic. You girls were off to school by then, and you were having babies of your own. How are your kids, anyway?"

"My daughter, and grandson, will be here for Holly Fest. My son is living in Massachusetts; he won't be home this year for Christmas."

"First year without your pa, too. That'll be hard. Good thing your sister will be here. I've had a chance to visit with her while she's staying with Thorny. They stop over for dinner. She's a lot different than when she was younger. Not so bratty." He laughed. Judd took the opportunity to stand and begin saying his good-byes for the evening.

Whistler set down his cup. Foster was standing on the ladder, placing the star atop the tree. Della was giving Whistler a hug and said, "Wait just a minute while we light the tree."

Foster scampered down the rungs, grabbed the plug-in end of the cord and asked, "Everyone ready?" We nodded as we stood in a semi-circle. I was holding my breath.

As he pushed the prongs into the socket a spark arched from the outlet. Foster flew back and the room went dark. Della gasped. Cricket shrieked. Peter began slapping at small flames that were marching up the drapery. I ran to Foster, "Are you okay?"

"Wow. What a jolt. What happened?"

Judd answered, "It appears that something shorted-out. As soon as we get some light in here, we can take a look."

Gunn pulled a flashlight from his pocket and cast the beam around, checking to see if all was well.

Peter, assured us that the fire was out, headed to the basement with Gunn to replace the fuse. There was light coming from the dining room and outside. *They must have been on different circuits*, I thought. Within second the lights came back on. Judd examined the electrical fixtures, "It looks like the extension cord you used has bare wires showing."

"I checked it earlier this morning," I said, "I checked all of them we were using."

I wanted to see for myself. "It looks like it's been cut." Judd agreed.

Della sat back in her chair, "That means, someone deliberately wanted to cause…" She trailed off.

I finished for her, "…a fire."

Cricket added, "Or they wanted someone to get electrocuted."

Della turned pale.

Before Judd began asking, I answered his question, "All four of the cousins knew we'd be decorating the tree tonight. Cricket and I told them. I forgot to call Moira, so she didn't know, unless one of the others told her."

Whistler said, "She and Thorny went to the city shopping today. They weren't home yet when I left to meet Macy after work"

Della turned toward Foster, "Are you okay?"

He nodded, "I'm fine. I've been shocked before; no biggy. Don't worry."

He got up from the floor and smiled at her, "I'm just sad that we can't see the tree all lit up."

Gunn said, "Sure we can." He had found another, safer cord and was putting it in place. He handed it to Foster, who still wanted to do the honors. He bent down and plugged it in. Della began to cry.

◆◆   **23**   ◆◆

All seem to say, throw cares away…

The next couple of days were a blur of red and green; sugar and sprinkles; wrap and ribbons. Final preparations for Holly Fest buried us in activity. It was an extremely joyful frenzy. In between tape and tags Della and I would talk about her family. During the stirring of sauces and pasta we had a nice visit with Lyda. Mabel sautéed both the meats and our curiosity about the summer parties held at the lodge. Priscilla checked and re-checked lists while noting some interesting history about the estate. The LaRonns were delivering supplies as well as furnishing tales of beach parties at *True North*. All and all the days were productive and informative. Della enjoyed the reminiscing. It was definitely beginning to feel like Christmas.

On the eve of the party, which happened to fall on the traditional festival of Yule, December 21, we gathered at the estate for a private little party. The next day would be teaming with children and families. There would be lots of commotion and excitement, and probably a sack full of tension being distributed by the cousins.

Cricket sat on the fireplace stoop warming her hands. Della was lighting the candles she had placed all around the room. I poured the wine after cautiously lighting the tree. We gathered around the oversized coffee table, sat on suede-like pillows and, in turn, each took a deep, relaxing breath. "This is nice," Della said.

"We needed a little time together," I added. Cricket ran her finger along the stem of the wine glass and said, "I think," she paused, "I think we should do something fun."

"Like what?" I asked.

"Maybe do a séance," her eyes sparkled.

"How about something a little less taxing?" Della suggested, "As much as I want to know what my dad may have to tell me, I'm not sure I can take any more stimulation."

I could see Cricket's enthusiasm dashed and I said, "Yule is a time for new beginnings. Is a séance really a good idea?"

"Probably not," she agreed, "but you can't blame a girl for trying?"

We laughed at her. She chuckled and said, "How about we just ask for a sign."

"You're relentless," Della said nudging her with her toe, "Okay, we can ask for a sign."

"From your dad?" Cricket persisted.

"Sure," Della agreed.

Cricket giggled, rubbed her palms together, and said, "We'd like a sign from Della's dad."

"That's it?" Della asked, "What would your séance consist of?"

I laughed, "She probably would have said, *Della's dad, if you're here, please appear.*"

The tree lights flickered. Our laughing stopped abruptly. I think my palms actually got sweaty.

They flickered again, as did all the twinkle-lights in the great room. And then they went out. Cricket mewed. Della said, "I'm so glad for the candles right now."

My heart beat was increasing, "Cricket, this was your idea. What now?"

"I don't know. I was just goofing around."

We heard a thump and a moan. We all scooted next to each other on the far side of the coffee table, away from the sound. A shadow loomed in the arched doorway that led toward the sunroom. As it leapt into the room we screamed and edged back toward the Christmas tree. Pine needles were prickling my back; at least I had hoped they were pine needles. The shrouded figure approached. Cricket was shaking. Then with one quick motion it raised its arms and said, "I am the ghost of Yuletime and I..."

We jumped up and tackled Foster. He laughed hysterically. So did we; after we stopped quaking.

"You got us good," I said. He was very pleased with himself and returned to the basement to replace the electrical fuse.

When he returned he was still laughing, "You guys are so predictable. I knew Cricket would want to see ghosts. That was fun." We didn't let him know, but it was rather entertaining.

After reiterating the scene a number of times the humor died down. Again, we sighed, in turn. The room became quite;

serene actually with the fire ebbing to a soft glow, candle flames flickering and the tiny Christmas lights peeking between branches. No one wanted to intrude on the peacefulness with the obvious concerns we were all sharing.

Finally, Cricket could not sit still any longer, "Are we ever going to find out the big secret that seems to be behind everything?"

Della forced a weary smile, "I don't know dear. I guess all will be revealed in time. Truth has a way finding its way home."

The night was waning. Embers were all that remained in the hearth. Candles had burned low. Della began snuffing them out. Foster was poking the ashes. I was repositioning pillows.

Cricket was standing by the doors to the den, "I think the clue to the will is on that bookmark," she said. As if on cue, a rumbling began in the den's fireplace. Cricket jumped. We gathered at the door and peered through the small, square panes of glass. Foster eased open the door. The room was filling with a light dusting of soot. A wheezy-wind sound was echoing down the chimney.

"I don't think its Santa," Foster said as he eased closer to the fireplace. We were lined behind him, moving footfall to footfall with him. The room suddenly went silent. Then, a thunderous sucking pulled all the sooty air back up the chimney. We waited. Nothing happened. It was over.

Cricket said, "There has to be something up that chimney. All the clues keep leading here."

I asked Cricket what she had said right before the noise started. She told me that she had a feeling that the bookmark held the answer to finding the will, and then she said it out loud.

"That was your sign," Della said, "and so is this." She pointed to the floor where the soot had formed a very distinctly shaped boot.

◆◆ 24 ◆◆

We'll frolic and play...jolly old St. Nicholas...chestnuts roasting o'er an open fire...grandma got run over by a reindeer...

Oh, the music that ran through my head as I bustled around my little cabin. It was a beautiful Holly Fest morning. A light snow had fallen during the night, and now the sun was cresting the pines. My family would be here in less than an hour. Just long enough for me to feed the cats and get outfitted in my holiday thermals.

They were right on time. Robert Marx is very punctual; Maggie tries to be. Dad and mom were bundled for a blizzard with snowpants that puffed and boots that thumped. Their jackets, scarves and headgear were crammed over layers of long underwear, sweaters and goose down vests. Mom wore her signature holiday pin; a Dalmatian with a red rhinestone ribbon. Dad had on his beaver-skin cap, complete with earflaps and matching choppers. They looked great. We hugged and hugged as if we'd not seen each other in a year, when it had only been last week. They loved my new life in Ottawa along with all the events that I volunteered for. Mom told me that my brother, Garrett, and his family would meet us at the big house.

We were the first to arrive at the lodge. Lights were plugged in; I told them to be careful and check cords first. Dad swept snow from the porch. Mom straightened the runners that were positioned throughout the lodge to protect carpets. All during their helpfulness, they were commenting on how beautiful Della's estate was and how perfect all the decorations were. It was wonderful to have them here.

Della arrived with her daughter and grandson. Jenny and I hugged. Mom squatted down by Joey. He said to her, "Santa's going to be here." He tucked close to her ear and whispered, "I'm going to ask for a puppy, mom doesn't know."

"It'll be our secret," she said quietly, then asked him, "What kind of puppy do you want?" He checked to see if his mom was looking and then poked a little finger at her coat pin, "A fire engine dog." Mom winked at me and mouthed, *isn't he cute?* I nodded.

Santa Claus is coming to town...

Cricket, followed by her folks, Art and Evie Bugsby, carried in boxes filled with refreshments, snacks and sweets. Grandma Maddy, with a food carrier in one hand and a cane in the other, clip clopped into the great room. "Ooooow, it's more splendid than ever. I'd forgotten how big it was in here." she said gawking from side to side. Cricket whispered to me, "It never crossed my mind that granny would have been a part of the old parties. I may have to drill her a bit."

Glad tidings we bring to you and your kin...

Jana, Cricket's sister arrived with the Beck family. She pulled me to the side, "Has the crazy lady showed up yet?" I shook my head no. She continued, "We saw her last night wandering around on the Red Earth road sniffing at the air, like one of Peter Holloway's hounds. After about twenty minutes her prissy sister hauled her back inside the motel. Mrs. Beck said that she'd done it before." I thanked her as she re-joined her friends.

Herb, Mabel and Pearl had closed up the Shipwreck and were toting pans of food through the side entrance. I grabbed a roaster filled with spaghetti from Pearl, "Merry Christmas Lexi. Isn't it a beautiful day?"

"It's holly, jolly all the way," I said while hoping that Foster and I had sufficiently cleaned up all the slippery wax. Mabel pined over the decorations while stacking trays of meats into the refrigerator. "It's lovely in here, dear," she said again and again. Herb and my dad talked fishing and weather while bringing in the last of the boxes. *All is merry and bright...*

Children squealed and laughed while making snow angels, snowballs and snow-sicles. A whistle blew. It was Bob McMahon's signal that the snowman contest was about to begin. "Where is Foster," I asked Cricket. She shrugged and scooted the LaRonn children over to the *Snowmaster.*

In the meadow we can build a snowman...

Bob lined the bundled kids up in pairs for the contest. The older ones would begin making the actual snowman, while the little ones would race up to him and gather snowman scarves, faces and hands which were laid out on blankets and stacked in bushel baskets. Bette was ready to help. The whistle blew. The cheering began. I looked around for Foster, he was nowhere in sight. Usually, he was right up front with his camera, clicking away.

Jana had her snow body built as Joey came running, his arms heaped with treasures. He stuck arms in the sides while Jana wrapped a big blue scarf around the frosty man. Together they placed a mouth made of corn and eyes of dried cornflowers. She held him up while he poked the carrot nose on his big man's face and plopped a hat on his icy head. Throwing their arms in the air they yelled, "Done!" They were the winners.

Bette handed Joey a small wooden toboggan and Jana a pair of white skates with pink pom-poms. She whispered to her, "They were my sister's, she loved to skate, but can't anymore. I hope you like them." Jana hugged her and ran to show Grandma Maddy.

I asked Bette where Foster was hiding. She winked at me and said that he had gone to Peter's. "What are they up to?" I asked.

She smiled and said, "I don't know, but he was up really early. So, it must be something important."

As I turned toward the lodge I saw the Greenes. They had all the children gathered on the porch. Anne was passing out cups of hot cocoa while Thomas held the audience spellbound with his animated storytelling. I remembered hearing him last year. He spun Native American tales of a bright star that led the way for lost children, and the great eagle who fought off wolves and returned a boy safely home though a terrible blizzard.

This year Thomas was telling of the big stag that carried the chief through the deep woods so he could bring food for the winter feast. Thomas wore his dark hair pulled back in long ponytail. His jacket was made of fur and leather, which he had said was bobcat and moose hide. Anne had on a fox fur parka trimmed with colorful cloth braid. As he finished his tale, Mabel, who had been waiting, called, "Food's ready!"

Some of the kids went back to playing while parents watched. Others filed into the lodge for the feast. I was all about the food at that moment. Lyda and Vivian had placed their hot-dishes alongside the others and were helping serve.

I found my parents chatting with Bob McMahon's brother Rourke and his wife Nora. I asked them when my brother would be arriving. Mom went through a long explanation of Garrett's schedule, which included watching Kaitlin's skating practice. "They'll be here soon," she ended.

As we headed for the food line I heard excited cheers from outside. It was too early for Santa's arrival. I wondered what was causing all the commotion. Cricket hollered, "Lexi come and see!"

Coming down the lane were two long lines of panting husky-type dogs followed by wooded sleds. Riding on the first one was none other than Foster. He was jingling bells and hollering Merry Christmas. Peter's pickup followed the procession. As the sleds skidded to a halt by the hitching post, Foster jumped off. He scanned the crowd until he spotted me. His smile grew wider and he laughed while motioning me over.

"Is this what you've been up to all morning?" I asked. He nodded while scratching one of the tethered dog's ears.

"Yep. Aren't they great? Peter knew some sled dog people and asked if they'd come for the day, and give rides!"

Children were being hoisted onto the sleds while the handlers, who had ridden over in a truck, top-heavy with a wooden dog box, maneuvered the dogs into position. The musher, a man of about thirty dressed in a down-filled parka and heavy fur mitts gave a command and off the team went back up the drive. The second sled was turned. Its driver was a woman, dressed nearly the same as her partner. When her riders were settled she said, "Hike!" And the dogs pulled forward.

We'll frolic and play the Eskimo way...

"Foster this great," I said as Peter, Della and Jenny came over by us.

"Where's Joey?" I asked.

"On the sled, with the dogs. He's absolutely giddy," Jenny said. Della smiled at Peter. He placed a gentle hand against her back, "I thought the boy might like it."

"You were right," she said. The first team was coming back. Peter and Foster went to help the handlers. My mom joined them. So did Gunn, who had arrived behind Peter's truck.

Cricket, who was holding a plate of food, said, "Santa has some competition this year. What time is Joe Hill bringing the jolly old man?"

"About mid-afternoon," I said, "Then he'll give sleigh rides again this year while the sun is setting. I love doing that."

After about an hour of sled dog rides, the mushers and canines needed a break. My dad, Gunn, Bob and Rourke stayed with the dogs that had been tied out at the edge of the yard toward my cabin.

While we had been outside, Thorny and the Old Timers' Band had set up in the corner of the great-room. Familiar melodies greeted us as we entered the lodge. The mushers joined us at the *Holly Feast Buffet*, as Mabel called it. While we ate, we were entertained by children dancing the polka and doing a youthful rendition of the jitterbug. My mom tapped my arm and asked, "Do you remember, when you were young, how we'd dance around the kitchen?"

Smiling, I said to her, "I wonder if I still know how to polka?" As the accordion played, we set aside our food and locked arms for a jostling whirl around the dance floor. We only made it through half the song, dressed in all our winter clothes, before needing to one-two-three back to our food.

Cricket had been clapping to the tune and laughed when we flopped into our chairs. "I remember doing the polka with my mom as a kid," she said, "we all had a kitchen dance hall growing up."

Some of the younger girls had changed from snowpants to frilly dresses. They twirled around the room to Rosemary Clooney singing, Suzy Snowflake.

Here comes Suzy Snowflake dressed in a snow white gown...

Grandma Maddy had clip-clopped over to Cricket. As she sat down, she said, "I remember when those old timers were young bucks playing their music at this big house. Those were the good old days."

Cricket elbowed me, "So granny, do you remember Della's dad, and his brothers?"

"Sure do. They were handsome fellows, especially Carsen. He was the nicest, too. If I wouldn't have been smitten by your granddad I might have thought him a fine catch."

The musicians began playing the Christmas Song as Cricket asked, "Do you remember Norville?"

"Sure do, he was the playboy of the group, always dancing with the ladies. His wife would get so angry. I remember one night, they had been drinking a whole lot, and she threw a whole tray of food at him. I'm not sure what happened, but she was having a tizzy fit over it. I suspected it was over a woman. He had that tendency. The other brother, the short one, he drank a lot, but was real quiet. His wife was a pretty woman, but rather plain, kind of like that daughter of theirs." She must have meant Beth Ann. I was going to ask her about the woman in the photo when I saw a procession making its way slowly toward us. It was the cousins.

Behind them were Whistler, Macy and Moira. I felt a shiver.

Cricket said "I smell trouble."

You better watch out...

I found Della to pre-warn her of their arrival. As we opened the door, the cousins were traipsing up the walkway. I whispered to Della, "Hope they don't fall off their heels." All four of them were wearing dresses; they must not have realized Holly Fest was a boots and snowpants affair. Small children skittered across the path. Snowballs sailed past them. The dogs were barking. The cousins looked irritated.

Before they reached the porch steps Della quietly said, "I can already feel their fury."

They should have thanked the Christmas spirits for Hazel. Without her they would have roasted in their own bitterness before reaching the door. Hazel was dressed in her bright red coat. She pranced right up to Della, gave her a peck on the cheek and said, "Happy Holly Fest cousin Della." It was one of the first normal things she had said since arriving in Ottawa, then she continued, "I lost my bracelet bunnies today. There were snakes on television, I don't like them. I like snow, do you?"

Blair squared her shoulders and said to Della, "I thought the party started at three o'clock? We thought we'd be early. I guess not."

Della informed her that Santa would be arriving at that time. The festival had started this morning.

Macy, who had been offering cheerful greetings to everyone said, "I had to work at the store, so grandpa and Moira waited for me. Everything looks spectacular." Whistler agreed. Moira was gazing around, taking in all the decorations and scanning the crowd. Della noticed that the cousins had begun shivering, so she graciously led the troop further into the lodge. Trudi or Beth Ann had not said a single word. This could be considered a blessing.

Silent night...

Beth Ann took off her gray wool and hung it on the coat rack. Trudi flung her hot pink jacket from her shoulders nearly knocking Whistler's glasses from his reddening face. Blair gave her black dress coat a neat patting as she placed it over her arm. Hazel struggled from her bright coat. As she did, Cricket's breath caught in her throat. She was wearing a powder blue polka-dot dress. It was styled with a 1950s belted waist and a full skirt that fell calf-length. It had tiny buttons up the front with a thin collar. Cricket pulled at me, "That looks just like the dress in that photograph."

"I know," I said, "where do you think she got it?"

"We could ask. I don't know if we'll get a straight answer, but hey, we can try."

Della had led them into the dining room and was serving up drinks.

I tried the direct approach, "Hazel, your dress is beautiful. Where did you get it?"

She was picking through frosted bells and stars. Blair answered for her, "She found it at the Goodwill Store, I think. I tried to get her to wear this darling cashmere sweater dress that I'd bought her, but she insisted on that one."

I was devising another angle of questioning when the entire place erupted, "Santa's here!" A deep *Ho Ho Ho* rang through the front door. There were squeals and shrieks as the kids bounded into the great room. Cricket skated, like a hockey pro, through the cheering mini-mob to escort Santa to his throne. She only upended a few of the frailer tots. A line was formed, of which Hazel filed into.

Most of the adults had gathered along the outskirts of the room with cameras, or food, in hand. A few of the teenage girls, including Mabel's grandniece Allysa, Bess McMahon, Kya Greene and Faith Beck were tiptoeing around in holly-green elf suits. Their duties were to hand the gifts to Santa, escort kids onto his lap and then return them to their parents. Jana, in her red velvet cap with white fur trim, was the head elf. She was positioned under the tree and in charge of gift distribution.

Music had changed from the accordion and fiddle to a guitar duet softly strumming carols. Above the tunes, everyone was chattering. While Santa's helpers were systematically moving each wiggling child back and forth, their tallest charge, Hazel, had wandered out of line.

Moira was eyeing her oddly; as was I. She was moving from person to person, sniffing her way through the crowd. Blair, who had been talking with Priscilla, spotted her sister. Excusing herself abruptly she nearly knocked over Elwood Waverly. She grabbed at Hazel's arm with a jerk just as she reached an elderly lady dressed in a tattered tan coat held snuggly with a deep red scarf.

Hazel whirled from her sister. Moira had eased closer to them; as had I, pulling Cricket along with me. Hazel was sniffing so deeply that her nostrils sucked into her face. Blair was trying to coax her back to Santa. The old woman was pushed against the wall and couldn't retreat from Hazel's crazy antics. In a complete turn-around, Hazel straightened her back, stopped sniffing and looked intensely into the woman's eyes. The old woman was obviously nervous. She picked at the sleeve of her jacket. Then tried to excuse herself. Hazel stepped into the woman's path while swatting Blair away.

I whispered to Cricket, "Who is she? There's something familiar about her."

"I don't know. I've seen her around a few times but never paid her much attention."

A low voice said from over my shoulder, "She's a ghost from the past."

We spun around to find Moira. At that moment, a small giddy laugh trickled from Hazel. She held her hands over her mouth. By now, Blair was forcible tugging at her disruptive sibling. Hazel was oblivious and kept wriggling from her grasp. More people were taking notice of the display. Finally, Hazel twisted around toward Blair. Her eyes grew dark and angry; a look I had not ever witnessed, coming from her sweet face.

She said rather loudly, through gritted teeth, "Let me go. I am talking with my mother."

◆◆ 25 ◆◆

There's bound to be talk tomorrow, at least there will be plenty implied...

That was a shocker.

Blair forced an uneasy laugh. Hazel glared at her.

By now Della and most of the adults had abandoned Santa and were focused on the back of the room.

The Christmas music continued to play and Santa was still *Ho Ho Hoing.*

Back here things weren't so merry.

Trudi nudged through and said, "What's she talking about, Blair?"

"Nothing. Just help me get her out of here."

"I'm not leaving," Hazel said and stomped her foot.

Beth Ann said, "Come on honey, we'll go get some ice cream."

"No."

The elderly woman was squirming away. She nearly cleared the door when a man, who had just emerged from the kitchen yelled, "Hey Mary, don't leave yet. There are lots of goodies. You have to try the Stollen." It was Joe Hill. He looked at *Mary*, and the rest of the stunned crowd. "What's going on?"

Mary ran out the door. Hazel had returned to Santa's line. Blair looked exasperated and embarrassed. Joe shrugged and went back into the kitchen. People began quietly chatting. Soon, the noise level had been restored through laughter and general gaiety. All seemed forgotten, but not by Cricket and me; or Moira. I turned to Della's sister and said, "What was that about? Who was that?"

Her eyes glinted at me as she said, "*Mary.*"

"I know that, but *Mary* who?"

Moira's red lips were glued tight and weren't divulging any information. I said, "We know that you're a P.I., the sheriff found the record of your license. We also know that you've been checking on things, too. What we don't know is where Hazel got that dress, who *Mary* is and why she just called her *mother*? Got answers? Want to share?"

All Moira said was, "Maybe later." She was through the crowd and out the door faster than Foster can eat cake; and that's fast. Blair had her jacket on and was stuffing Hazel into hers. Jana had sent an elf over to Hazel with a present and she was giddy with glee.

You'll go down in history...

Whatever had gone through Hazel's mind had obviously passed and she was as cheery as any crazy grown kid at Christmas.

As the four cousins gathered at the front door, Della made her way politely through the guests. Reaching her cousins, I could hear her coaxing them to stay. Hazel was begging not to leave. She wanted to dance. Beth Ann, who was fussing with her hair clasp, shyly stated that she hadn't a chance to eat, or visit yet. Trudi rolled her eyes, gesturing a noncommittal *whatever*. As for Blair, she finally succumbed, removed her coat and followed Hazel upstairs.

I turned to Cricket, "I remember. The old woman, she's the face I saw in Hazel's mirror. We have to find out who she is."

"Joe Hill obviously knows, lets ask him." We re-bundled ourselves and high-tailed it to the hitching post. The sled dog teams were gone, and so was the horse-drawn sleigh. My dad was the only thing parked at the wooden rail. "Dad, where did Joe go?"

"He said he had to run an errand."

"Is he coming back? Was there anyone with him?"

"He didn't say, and there was a woman with him. Why?"

I explained what had happened inside the lodge. He looked at me rather curiously, "Do you think these things are all tied to the missing will?"

"Possibly, but I don't really understand how."

He told me that my brother had called. Kaitlin had twisted her ankle at skating practice and they wouldn't be coming. "He was very disappointed."

I was feeling disheartened, too. Cricket nudged my arm. As I turned I saw Lyda, Warren and Vivian leading Elwood to their truck. Before we could say goodbye they were gone. Cricket whispered, "Mr. Waverly looked real upset. And Lyda never leaves before the fireworks. What is going on?"

"Maybe he was sick, or tired," I offered. But I had to concur with Cricket, something wasn't right.

Santa was retreating out the front door, waving with a *Merry Christmas to all.* Heading down the path he gazed around for his get-away sleigh and driver, which had left with *Mary.* Gunn showed up to chauffer Santa, aka, Sheriff Judd Golden in his tin -sleigh. My dad sat shotgun.

Cricket and I stood by ourselves at the hitching post. "Where did Moira go?" she asked.

I shook my head trying to rattle some answers into place, "I don't know, and I didn't think I'd ever say it, but I'll be glad when Holly Fest is over. I wonder how Della is doing."

We found her paging through old photo albums encircled by over half the guests, at least those over forty. The kids were upstairs playing with their new toys, and probably a few of the old ones. Herb and Art were cleaning the kitchen so that the ladies could visit, or so they had said. Cricket and I knew it was their chance to sneak a bit of high-octane nog.

""Where is Foster?' I asked.

"Maybe he left with the sled dog people."

"This is all so crazy. I thought we'd be having a wonderful family holiday."

"Some families aren't as great as ours."

"I know, but even mine didn't all show up."

Foster emerged from the den. "Is the food gone? I really worked up an appetite."

I tugged him toward the kitchen, "What were you doing?"

"I pulled the cameras and downloaded the pictures."

Cricket, ready for more excitement, asked, "What did you find out?"

"I thought I'd catch one of the cousins in the act. Instead every last one of them had been snooping around, including Della."

"What?" I said.

"Yep, she was leafing through her dad's files and attacking the bookcase. They're not video cams, just still-shots, so it was hard to get all the movements. Moira was here, too. It was strange. On every frame she was just standing, almost posing."

We finagled some sandwich meats, bread and pickles from the nog-drinkers in the kitchen. As we took up seats around the table I filled him in on Hazel's escapades.

"Do you think she really thought that was her mother?" he said with a mouth full of ham and rye, "Didn't her mother commit suicide?"

I handed him a napkin and said, "No that was the woman her dad was going to marry, right?"

Cricket thought it over and said, "Maybe they both did?"

"This is so confusing," I said grabbing a pickle spear with vengeance.

And if you ever saw it, you'd even say it glowed...

A voice from the great room announced, "Fireworks in twenty minutes." It was my dad. The volunteer firefighters must be ready for their part in the festival. We went out onto the front deck of the lodge where Foster and Peter had shoveled off huge drifts of snow. Bundled for the nippy night air we huddled close together in chairs and on benches. There was a boom. The sky over Lake Superior lit up with a gigantic frosty white, sparkling snowflake. The oowws and aahhs began. Winter fireworks glittered in the cold. Over the years we've learned to keep them spectacularly short or we end up with frost bitten spectators.

After the grand finale of five white icy cascades, five red poinsettias and five great green bursts, guests began retreating to the warmth of the lodge. My parents took their leave due to the long drive home. Mom, giving me a big hug, told me to tell Della she'd check on the puppy for Joey. Dad kissed the top of my head and tucked some cash into my hand telling me to use it for the gas tank when I come home on Christmas Eve. I accompanied them to the door and watched as they walked arm in arm along the lantern-lit path.

The high school choir had lined up along the side wall. After everyone shook off the chill from the outside show, they settled in for the next Holly Fest performance. Looking around, I noticed that Della and Peter were seated by her family. Cricket was holding grandma Maddy's hand. Foster had his niece on his lap. Lyda and Warren had returned. Like other couples, they had their arms draped around each other's shoulders. Families huddled together as the choir began Hark the Herald Angels Sing with a soft, low, *ooh ooh ooh.*

I suddenly felt very alone. Tears were welling in my eyes. I backed up toward the door to the den and bumped into someone. It was Judd. I smiled empathetically up into his kind face. Resting my head on his shoulder, he patted my arm. Gunn moved to my other side and rested a comforting hand on my waist.

The choir ended their concert with *We Wish You a Merry Christmas.* Everyone clapped and cheered like proud grandparents, which some of them were.

A new group of musicians took over the corner staging area. Included in the band were the owners of the Loose Moose. Rather than playing holiday jingles, they reflected back to the lodge's original days, setting the mood with tunes from the forties and fifties. Cricket was delighted. While the band was warming up, Mabel brought snacks from the kitchen. Cricket and I took the opportunity to sneak away to my cabin to change into era-friendly dancing attire.

◆◆ **26** ◆◆

I'm dreaming of a white Christmas, just like the ones I used to know...

We slipped into the old fashioned dresses we'd borrowed from Priscilla. She told us that even though they were part of the museum's costume closet; they had actually belonged to her and her sister. Cricket twirled around as sparkling fuchsia taffeta billowed out in a stiff circle. She tugged at the strapless bodice before tucking her arms into a matching jacket with three-quarter sleeves and a big rhinestone studded button.

"This dress is dreamy," she twirled again and then curtsied, "I feel like a movie star. And you look like one, wow!"

I stood in front of my mirror, staring at the transformation that took place. "Amazing isn't it that we *are* women, once we peel off all that wool and long underwear."

I adjusted the thin white straps that held up yards of crisp fabric flecked with golden glitter. Cricket was tugging up the zipper that strained at my waist. "You're thin. They must have been starved!" She added, "I wonder how Hazel ever fit into her dress."

After finally fastening the elegant dress to my body, I draped an ultra soft white fur stole over my shoulders and clipped the sides together with a glitzy broach fashioned from brilliant amber stones. Soft, white gloves completed my ensemble. We fluffed our hair, dabbed on some perfume and were ready for our first gala party at *True North*.

"I'm so excited," Cricket kept repeating. With high heels in hand, we pulled on our boots and wrapped our heavy coats over our shoulders.

Everyone dancing merrily in a new old-fashioned way!

Enchanting swing tunes greeted us as we made a grand entrance into the room. Others had changed into festive dresses, including Della. She waltzed over to us in a darling, fern-green chiffon with layers of matching lace and silk. "You look fabulous," we all intoned to each other. "I found this upstairs," Della whispered, "Isn't it divine? Let's dance."

We followed her through twirling women and men shuffling to a lively jitterbug.

The music slowed to a waltz. Foster held out his hand and with a bow asked, "May I have this dance?" He looked debonair in a starched white shirt and gray slacks.

"I think I have an opening on my dance card," I giggled while taking his hand. As we danced I realized that he'd combed back his usually unruly hair. He was perfectly styled for the era, minus the pencil-thin mustache. The night was turning out to be magical. That was until the cousins tipped a bit too much holiday cheer.

You better watch out...

Of course it was Trudi who had to make a scene. I wasn't sure what she was ranting over, but she was definitely causing a ruckus. As I got closer, I saw that her hot-pink, skin tight sheath was spattered with dark red wine. At least I had hoped it wasn't blood. Verbal chastising was spewing from her drunken mouth. It was aimed toward Blair.

Della was trying to calm her, when Blair grabbed Trudi's arm before she could begin retaliating with a reversed wine bath. Both women were screaming and swearing. Beth Ann was trying to coax Trudi toward the den when they stumbled and a pink handbag inadvertently decked Blair.

Bolting from behind a large man in suit, Hazel jumped at Trudi, screaming "Don't you hit my sister!" The sheriff stepped in to grab the crazy lady. Peter held tight to Blair while Gunn was left with Trudi.

The whole scene only lasted minutes, but it took considerably longer to restore a semblance of civility. Trudi could not shut her mouth, Hazel was crying, Blair was frothing with vulgarities while Beth Ann kept mumbling.

The band played on. Murmurs could be heard of how the offspring were just like parents, and the apples don't fall far from the trees. Grandma Maddy, speaking a little too loudly said, "You can sure tell which one is Norville's kid; bad temper." Blair spun around and was about to orally accost her when Cricket rose to within an inch of Blair's face. Cricket's girth, accented by the sheer volume of her dress was enough to quaff the women's words without Cricket's threat, "Don't you dare say one syllable to my grandmother."

Blair spun around and aimed for another glass of wine. Trudi already had a refill in her hand. They positioned themselves at opposite sides of the room. We took up posts as Holly Fest police. "They sure are scrappy," Gunn said to his cousin, the sheriff, who replied, "Could get brutal after a few more cocktails."

Della chimed in, "Let's hope not."

Cricket added, "I wonder if the old parties were like this?"

"That's not what I remember, but I was young, so they could have been," Della replied while keeping watch on her family, and then asked, "I wonder where Moira went?"

I told her, we had figured she went looking for Joe Hill and his passenger, *Mary*. This made more sense now that we knew she was a detective.

After another hour of dancing, guests began thinning. Della took up hostess station at the front entrance bidding each farewell and happy holidays. Many hugs were exchanged along with gracious compliments.

Jenny took Joey back to the Belle Star Lighthouse Inn. The kitchen crew had cleared out for the night after storing most of the leftover food. The band packed their equipment. A few stragglers, including Priscilla were dancing out the front door.

The cousins were seated at the dining table around a tray of cheese and crackers. They were still drinking. Amazingly, they were conversing amicably among themselves, except for Hazel who was still upstairs *playing*. I plopped on the sofa. Foster took up a seat next to me and Cricket next to him. Peter and Della sat on another of the overstuffed couches. Judd took up his post on Santa's chair. Gunn leaned against the door jamb to the den with a toothpick in his mouth and a watchful eye trained at the dining room.

Just when we thought the evening had concluded, and all Christmas carols departed from my mind, a black caped figure emerged from the sun porch entrance.

With all of the folks at home...

"Well kids, it looks like the party has wound down," Moira said as she set down on the sofa's arm. Tired as I was, I hoped she was here to give an explanation. She did, sort of; in her own way and in her own time.

"I followed Joe Hill and his passenger home," she began, "He stopped by his place to exchange his horse for his Ford and then continued past the farm. There are miles of land in Joe Hill Hollow and I didn't think anyone lived beyond his place."

Cricket sat up, "There's a couple summer homes down that road."

"That's what I had thought," Moira said, taking off her cape, "I waited until he had returned and then drove down there to see for myself. At the end of his property line, by the far fencing, there's a tiny cabin. There was a light on, so I could easily see into the windows. Want to guess who I saw?" She looked at me, so I responded, "*Mary?*"

Moira nodded, "Does anyone know who she is?"

"Is this another rhetorical question?" I asked. She shook her head, no. We all did the same. No one had a clue.

Noise began to rise from the dining room. Della sighed, "Here we go again."

Moira asked her what she meant. Explaining to her sister the earlier escapes of their family, she added, "I wish they'd go."

Moira said with a wink, "Ah, this could be fun. Let's see if we can rile then up a bit."

The sheriff advised against it, but Moira goaded them on, "What's all the commotion about girls? I missed the first round, are you going to duke it out again?"

Trudi was the first to storm into the great-room. Drink in hand, she slurred, "You just stay out of it. I have half a mind to pop you!"

Moira, enjoying the ruse, said "You're right about that Trudi; you only have half a mind."

They highball glass would have come sailing across the room if Beth Ann wouldn't have snatched it away. Blair strode in heavy steps halfway across the room and called loudly for Hazel.

Moira began in a steady pace, "There are few things I'm curious about. It seems you've all been sneaking around the estate. What are you looking for?"

She stopped and stared at the three of them. They teetered a bit then Beth Ann spoke in an overly exaggerated voice, "No we haven't."

Moira shot back at her, "Yes you have."

"No we haven't," she said even louder.

Blair waved a hand, "Oh for Pete's sake, yes we have. I fell on those damn stairs and got a nasty bruise."

She looked at Peter, "Thank you, Mr. Hemingway, for fixing them."

Trudi was not going to be left out, "I was here, too. So was Beth Ann."

"Trudi be quite."

"No, I have every right to be here and so do you. I'm tired of being treated like criminals. Maybe they should clear out. Either way," she continued, as the volume in her voice rose, "I want the money from this place. I want my share. I deserve a third, I mean a … whatever… my share."

Blair cut her off, "I've heard enough. I'm leaving. Hazel, Hazel let's go. Where is that girl?"

"Right here!" Dressed in layers of frilly clothes and a stained white summer hat she spun into the room. The garments looked wet and wrinkled. Blair looked mortified. Grabbing at the brim of her hat, Hazel said, "Do you like it? I found it hiding in the attic."

◆◆ 27 ◆◆

From now on our troubles will be out of sight…

It was a stumbling rush as the cousins aimed for the exit. Mumbling and grumbling mingled with Hazel's anxious chattering about the attic. Blair tugged her sister's jacket over her many layers of dress-up clothes while maneuvering her out the door. Beth Ann was the last to leave and the only one to say goodbye.

After a moment of sheer silence, Moira walked over to Foster and said, "Did I look good on those pictures?"

He squirmed a little.

"What pictures?" Della asked.

Her sister answered, "The ones your young detective took with his sensor cameras."

"How did you know?" Foster was curious.

"They make an ever so slight hum when the photo is taken. Most people can't differentiate between the camera and say, the refrigerator, or furnace. But I can."

"You are good," he said.

"Sometimes," she replied, "but there is something that has me stumped." She pulled a piece of paper from her pocket and enfolded it. She looked at Della and said, "I have tried to make sense of this message from dad, but it has me puzzled."

"The bookmark!" Della said, "You took it. What does it say?"

Moira scooted in between her sister and Peter handing the yellowing slip of letterhead paper to Della. We couldn't refrain. All of us moved behind her on the couch. Her hands were beginning to shake, as was her voice.

The note read:

Time can push what a brick can't move, on what is left;
A man six foot tall rows his boat up a stream to the river;
Rows the ship in.

A smile as bright as a Christmas star appeared on Della's face while tears streamed down her cheeks.

In between giddy laughs she said, "I know what it says. I know where the duplicate will is!"

Della pointed at her dad's writing and told Foster to get a paper and pen.

She began reading aloud, one word at a time, "Push...brick...on...left...six ...rows...up...two...rows...in."

"How the hell did you know that?" Moira asked in dismay.

"Dad and I would sit on the docks and read shipping crates. We'd say every third word and make silly sentences." She looked at her sister, "You were home with mom or off with your friends. You didn't like the docks, remember?"

"I remember. Mostly I didn't like the stench of fish and oil. And, it was filthy. It made me sick."

She pointed back at the note, "What bricks does he mean?"

Cricket answered quickly, "The ones in the den."

Moira looked at her inquisitively, "And you know this, how?"

Cricket opened her mouth, but before she could say anything, I nonchalantly kicked her leg. She closed her lips and shrugged. Moira gave her a suspicious look, and then turned her gaze to her sister. Della sighed and told her about the air gusts from the chimney and the soot descending on us. She left out the hovering black ball and the boot shape on her compact.

"Okay then," Moira said, "Let's check-out the chimney." We moved into the den.

Peter offered to do the dirty work and reach up the chimney. He counted up six and two to the left. He pushed on the brick. Nothing happed.

Cricket was squatted next to him, "Push harder." He did.

On the bookshelf next to the fireplace a section of shelving creaked forward. Judd and Gunn firmly tugged at it. It inched outward. After another eight inches it was apparent that it needed to be hoisted sideways. Peter and Foster were helping redirect the massive section of wood and books.

Neatly hidden in the wall was a safe. Moira inspected it, "It appears that we need a key."

Cricket heaved a sigh and said, "Now what do we do?"

I tapped Della's shoulder, "I think you found some keys, remember?"

She ran for her purse and returned jingling a set of mismatched keys. As she handed them to Moira, she said, "Maybe one of these will work."

Moira scanned the keys, fingered a small brass one and carefully fit it into the lock. It clicked and opened. Inside, a second fireproof steel door barred our entrance. This one was equipped with a combination lock.

"Can you magically pull the combination out of your sack, too?" she asked.

Della crossed her arms over her chest and said, "No, I supplied the key. Maybe you can magically supply the numbers."

Moira's bright red lips smirked at her sister. She scrutinized the faces in the room, settling her stare on the sheriff. Giving him a look of defiance, she said, "What the hell, give me some room, and keep quiet."

She placed her ear next to the steel safe and began slowly turning the dial. After only a few moments I heard a soft click. Moira pushed down on the handle and the door popped open. The interior of the safe was dark. Before I could produce my little flashlight, Moira beat me to the light. A bright blue beam eerily illuminated the metal.

There was a small metal box sitting atop a manila envelope. Moira reached in and pulled them out. She handed the box to Della and began opening the envelope's clasp. She laid the contents on the coffee table. Della set the box next to the paperwork and said, "Let's see what's hidden in here that made Blair feel the need to steal the original."

Moira looked at her sister, "How did you figure out it was Blair?"

"Foster helped. He had a print out of her client list. When I went to the office I recognized the secretary's name. She had opportunity, now I'd like to see what the motive was?"

"That's good," Moira looked a Foster, "I didn't think you had that figured out."

Foster blinked his eyes at her, "On my way to a big truck," he said. She laughed.

I was getting anxious. Cricket was worse. She looked as if she could rip into the documents at any minute.

Moira scanned each sheet and then handed it to Della. She stopped, held one out for her sister to see and said, "Well, well, here it is. I suspected as much, but now there's proof." Della gasped.

"What?" We all asked.

Della seemed stunned. She stared at the paperwork on her lap and said, "*True North* does not get split between the six of us; just two."

"Who?" Cricket said, again ready to rip the page away from her.

Moira took over for her, "It seems that our two uncles, before they died, decided that their daughters needed the cash rather than the property. I have watched our cousins' finances for many years and had always suspected it but, here it is in black and white."

"What are you saying?" Judd asked, a little behind on all the information we had gathered.

Della answered, "The property belongs to Moira and me. I wonder if the cousins even knew."

"I don't think so," Moira said, "They may have guessed it. Blair obviously read it when she fingered the will."

Foster stood and began pacing, "That would explain some of those larger deed transactions we found on record. It also explains were Trudi and Beth Ann got their initial wealth. It's possible that they knew about the sale years ago from their father and that they told Blair and encouraged her to steal the will."

"That's possible," Moira said.

"I don't think that's what happened," Cricket said in a quiet voice. We stared at her. It was very uncharacteristic of Cricket to use a hushed voice. She was holding the manila envelope in one hand and a small sheet of paper in the other. "I think this is the reason Blair stole the will." She passed the piece of paper to Della and Moira. "Well I'll be damned," Moira said. Della gasped, again. Their eyes met. "What do we do?" Della asked.

Moira said, "I think we should gather them together, tell them about the will and see what happens from there. Maybe Blair will fess-up."

Cricket added, "Or maybe she'll try to destroy the evidence and us with it."

◆◆ **28** ◆◆

Come they told me…

On Moira's advice, and the sheriff's, the cousins were not told that the duplicate will had been found. Instead Della called a family meeting.

Two by two they arrived at the estate. The first words out of Trudi's mouth were not a congenial good morning, but rather, "What are they doing here? They're not family." She pointed at me, Foster, Cricket, Judd and Peter. I had to admit, she had a point. Della spoke up with Moira standing firmly behind her, "I asked them to join us. It involves them, too."

Trudi continued, "I don't see how? I think you are just bullying us."

Moira spoke, "Just sit down." Trudi harrumphed onto the sofa. Beth Ann sat next to her and placed her hands neatly on her lap.

Cricket brought coffee and leftover cakes. Jenny helped her serve while Foster kept Joey busy playing with his new toys. Hazel went over and sat with them by the tree. Blair positioned herself into a chair near to Hazel.

Moira held up the manila envelope, "It seems that we have found a copy of the missing will."

I watched their reactions. Blair hid her concerns rather well. Her eyes were fixed on the envelope. Her lips were locked. Her one eye gave her away as it twitched.

Trudi, while continuing to play with her puffy scarf said, "Halleluiah, now we can get on with things." Beth Ann began to fidget with her buttons. I think she knew more than we had given her credit for. Sheepishly, she said, "What does it say?"

Moira handed each of them a copy, and said, "It says that your fathers sold their share of the estate to our dad. That means you do not have any claim to *True North*."

Trudi stared at the paper in her hands and then erupted, "That can't be true. You made it up, forged these papers. I don't believe it. I'll get a lawyer. I want my share."

Moira was ready for her, "You already *had* your share. When your dad passed away, you received quite a sizeable cash settlement. Correct?"

Trudi would not back down, "That was from the sale of the business. That's what dad said."

Beth Ann was trying to whisper to her, but Trudi pushed her away. Moira looked at Beth Ann, "Did you have something to say?"

Beth Ann, who was nearly twisting her buttons from her jacket said, "I have often wondered why the cash amount was so large. I knew what the shipping business had been worth. I had hoped that it was extra investments that had raised the inheritance."

Trudi looked at her, "Just be quiet. Dad's finances are none of their concern. I think they tampered with these documents. Where did you find them anyways?"

Della explained about the hidden safe, and informed her cousins that all the paperwork was notarized and completely legal. Moira ready to put Trudi on defensive said, "Maybe you and Beth Ann knew about the sale and stole the will, hoping to insure the six-way split?"

At this comment, Blair unclenched her lips slightly.

Trudi, who was getting redder by the minute, said, "Don't be absurd. We figured Blair stole it."

Blair laughed uncomfortably. Moira asked, "Why would you say that?"

Trudi and Beth Ann exchanged looks. They did not respond. I could tell Moira was struggling for a way to have the

information from the small piece of paper exposed without
having to just blurt it out.

As planned, I said, "I would like to know who stole the
framed photograph of the woman with the powder blue polka-
dot dress. It looked like the same dress Hazel was wearing
yesterday. Was it?"

No one said a word so I continued, "We'd like to know
who poured wax on the floor the other night and slit Della's
tires?"

Moira spoke, "Someone did that?"

I nodded, and then continued, "I think each of you was
looking for the duplicate will. I think Trudi took the photo, and
I think she also has been sabotaging us. Am I correct?"

I had known blaming Trudi would get her talking.

"That's absurd! I was inside talking with Della when her
tires were slashed and when you guys slipped on that wax. It
couldn't have been me."

"Then it must have been your sister," I said, "because I
never said when Foster and I *slipped* on the wax."

Beth Ann piped up, "You don't have any proof."

Judd spoke for the first time, "I'm afraid we do. You
bought the knife at Ottawa Outfitters and Roy remembered.
We compared the cuts made in the tires with the knife style
you purchased. They matched."

"That's not conclusive," she said gaining more momentum
than she had ever shown. "There are many hunting style
knives purchased at that store. You're searching, and stretch-
ing circumstantial evidence."

"Actually m'am, I'm not," Judd continued, "The knife you
purchased was handmade, and there are only two like it. Nice
choice by the way. Roy still has one of them, and you purchased the other. We'll be talking before you leave town."

Beth Ann began to cry, "Why couldn't you just leave us alone?"

"That was another of my questions," I said, "Who made a threatening phone call to me the other night? It sounds like it was you Beth Ann."

She was still crying, "Go ahead, blame me for everything, even taking the will, it doesn't matter. I don't have anything. It's all gone and I'm getting older, so what difference does it make. I did it all."

Moira looked at me, then Della. We were confused. We knew she hadn't taken the will. Obviously Blair, to protect her little secret, was willing to let her cousin take the rap. Moira got a gleam in her eye, and said, "Did Blair pay you to confess?"

Beth Ann stopped crying so abruptly it was a clear sign of admission. She sniffed a few times, regaining her weeping composure and said, "Whatever do you mean, I told you, I did it. I did it all."

"I don't believe you," Moira said.

"Too bad," Beth Ann retorted.

Della said, "I didn't want it to come to this. I had hoped you would be truthful. But,…" She reached into the envelope and pulled out the small sheet of paper.

As Della held it out, as if to better read the document, Blair lunged at her, "Give me that!"

She would have gotten her hand on it except Jenny leaped between her mother and her aunt. Blair tried to push past her. She was hissing, "Give me that now. You have no right to it." She was becoming so forceful that Judd and Peter had to grab her by the arms to restrain her. Blair's eyes were like fire balls, she was yelling, "That is no one's business but mine. Give it to me!"

Moira said, "On the contrary, it is someone else's business. It's Hazel's."

Blair continued to writhe, "I am her guardian. I make the decisions for her. You have no right! How can you be so cold?"

Della, trying to calm her, said, "You think you're doing the best thing, but maybe she has the right to know. There are more people involved in this. Maybe Lyda would like to know, too?"

Before another word was said, the kitchen door opened. Lyda appeared, "Did I hear my name? I was picking up some dishes from last night and, I was trying not to eavesdrop, but you were yelling awfully loud. Then I heard my name." As she came closer, she said, "What might I like to know?"

Blair reeled from her restrainers and grabbed Hazel, "We're leaving. You should've let this die with our dads."

Moira loomed over her cousin, "Can old lies die? Sometimes ghosts need to be brought into the light. It's the only way they're set free. It's time Blair."

She sank to the floor by Hazel. "I've tried to protect her all these years."

"You were trying to protect your family name," Moira said.

"Well, yes," Blair spat at her, "wouldn't you?"

Moira glanced at Della with a look, *would they have done the same*.

Lyda spoke up, "What's going on?"

I brought her over by me and sat her on the sofa, and said, "We found Carsen True's will, and there were some other documents with it; one in particular."

Blair let out a primal grunt, "Enough. Let me tell it. If it has to come out, I'll be the one giving the explanation, not some outsider." Della was going to speak up. I shook my head.

Blair patted Hazel's hand and began pacing. She stopped in front of Lyda, "You were only a little girl. Your daddy thought the sun rose and set on your smile. Your mama knew this. She began to live in your shadow. She wanted to be happy for you, but she was tired of never getting any attention from your dad. I remember that summer. I was only here for a week, before going back to my friends at school. Your mom was at the estate every day." She paused and crossed over to the big windows. "She had said that she was cleaning, but I saw it differently. I imagine my mom had, too."

She turned back toward us, "Nine months later, without ever knowing my mom was pregnant, Hazel was born into our family. I put it all together, but never said a word to anyone."

Lyda wrinkled up her face and said, "What are you saying?"

Blair turned to her, "I'm saying, your mama had a baby with my daddy."

Lyda inhaled and turned white. Blair flopped into a chair and stared at Della and Moira, "There it's out. Are you pleased?"

Della blushed. Moira didn't.

Lyda looked at Hazel, "Does that mean Hazel and I are sisters?"

"Half-sister," Della said gently, "and there's more."

Blair hid her head in her hands. Della continued, "We found a photo in the attic of your mom with Norville True, she was wearing a powder blue dress."

Lyda said, "With polka dots; I remember it vaguely." She gasped, "It looked like the dress Hazel was wearing yesterday. Where did she get it?"

Cricket jumped in, unable to refrain any longer, "From your mother."

"What do you mean?" Lyda asked, "My mother's been gone for years. I don't understand?"

"We don't understand all of it either," said Della, "You may have to ask your dad in order to get all of the background. What we do know is that Meredith Mackenzie Waverly had a baby with Norville True. We have the birth certificate. The rest, we pieced together. There was a woman here yesterday. She has had contact with Hazel. She lives out past old Joe Hill. Her name is Mary Maki. We belief her real name is Meredith Mackenzie Waverly; your mother."

Hazel, who had seemed to be playing and not paying attention stood up and said, "Mary is my mother. She gave me the blue party dress. She smells like honeysuckle." She fumbled beneath her creamy yellow sweater and produced a locket. She said, "I took this from her. She had it around her neck." *Larceny runs in the family*, I thought.

She opened it up and said, "Mary told me that these are pictures of me and my sister." She showed Della, and said looking at Blair, "The baby is me and the other girl is my sister. I don't understand, you have dark hair and this girl has red hair."

Blair looked longingly at her unable to give an explanation. Lyda touched her auburn hair, and said to Hazel, "Can I see the picture?"

Hazel showed it to her and said, "Mary said she never takes it off. Maybe I should give it back to her." She looked at Blair, "Can we take it back to Mary?" Blair nodded. Then Hazel turned and went back to playing Lincoln logs with Joey.

Trudi and Beth Ann had been very quiet. Finally Trudi spoke up, "I knew something was fishy. Beth Ann had asked Blair to find out about the will. I heard them talking one day. They mentioned the Red Earth Road. They were being all secretive. Now it all makes sense."

"Is that why you were on that road?" I asked Trudi.

"Well yeah, I wanted to see if I could figure out what they were talking about."

Blair looked at her, "We were talking about the motel, nothing else. You are so stupid."

Trudi gathered a rebuttal, "No I'm not. You're the one who got caught."

Beth Ann spoke up, "Trudi, you don't know what you're talking about. I had no idea about Hazel and neither did you. It's over. We don't have any of dad's money left and there's no more coming in. We're on our own."

Moira looked at Beth Ann, "Actually, you did know about Hazel. You've been blackmailing Blair for years and hiding the money from your sister. I accessed your overseas account after noticing that Blair was paying the exact same amount to an unknown source, every month for eleven years."

Trudi looked at her, "Is that true? Eleven years you've been getting money? And hiding it from me?"

Beth Ann didn't answer, Moira did, "That was about the time your dad died, wasn't it Beth Ann. He told you the secret and you used it against Blair. He also told you that he'd sold the estate, too. You knew all of this and never told Trudi, right? Then, when Carsen passed away you knew it may all come out. That's why you set-up to have the will stolen through Blair. You didn't want your funds to stop. And you didn't want your sister to find out. You also found out about Mary Maki, thanks to your old sweetheart Marcus Thorndike. Then, you had even more dirt on Blair. That was very smart of you, but not smart enough."

Blair had started crying. Trudi was looking at her sister with disgust. Lyda was in quiet shock. Jenny had her arm around her mom. Moira said, "Anything else?"

The cousins were looking at their laps as if some mysterious writing might appear and make everything better. It didn't happen. Instead, Della said, "I do have something I'd like to add on a merrier note. Moira, Jenny and I had our own family meeting earlier this morning after finding out about the property. We decided, actually because of Trudi's idea; that we'd like to share the estate with the town of Ottawa rather than keep it as our private piece of real estate."

Trudi glared at Della, "We don't really care about your plans unless we're cashing in on it."

Della looked embarrassed for her cousin. I spoke up, "I'd like to hear." Cricket nodded and Foster joined us, leaving Joey to play with Hazel.

"Thanks," Della said, "We are going to turn the estate into a bed and breakfast."

Jenny took over, "Mom, Joey and I will be moving here. We've talked about adding a community swimming pool and a mini-golf course on the estate." She looked at her mom and smiled.

Della looked at me, "Lexi, you can keep your cabin for as long as you like."

Again Trudi interrupted, "Great, she gets a cabin and I get nothing."

Beth Ann swiveled toward her sister and said, "That's enough. I think it's time *you* knew the truth, too." Trudi looked at her indignantly.

Beth Ann continued, "You should be glad you got your share of this estate in the first place. Dad was generous enough to give it to you."

"What are you talking about?"

"There were more than two birds sneaking around the bushes back then. While Norville was keeping company with Lyda's mom, her dad was doing the same with our mom. You see dear sister; you too are the product of a summer fling. We are half sisters and I have been protecting you, and this family name, for years."

"Oh my God," Lyda said, "Trudi is my sister, too?" And she fainted.

◆◆ **29** ◆◆

Thou bidst us true and faithful be...

It was as quite as a funeral procession when the four cousins left the estate.

Lyda was returning home to seek answers from her dad.

"I think it was just too much for her to bear," Cricket said, "Finding out that both her parents were cheating on each other, her mother was still living in Ottawa and that she not only had a crazy sister, but also a nasty one, too."

"I shouldn't laugh," I said, "but it is kind of bizarre."

"All this made me hungry," Foster said. Gunn came in from the kitchen hauling a heaping plate of sandwiches. He had been hiding out, just in case extra protection was needed.

"What will happen now?" Cricket asked.

Judd told her that charges would be brought up against Blair and Beth Ann. Trudi, he felt, had gotten her just rewards: nothing.

While everyone was hashing over the hodgepodge of details, Della took me off to the side. "Moira and I had a long talk last night about Thorny and Marcus, our parents and our lives. We sorted out many things, including some of the secrets that had kept us distant for many years."

"I'm so happy for you, and that Jenny, Joey and you will be moving up here. By the way my mom is checking on that p-u-p-p-y for Christmas."

Moira was relaying a bit of history about Beth Ann and Marcus that Thorny had spilled years ago while emptying a whiskey bottle. I whispered to Della that I had noticed Beth Ann's hair barrette at the party, maybe it was Marcus she had been waving to.

Foster asked Moira about the tape recorders. She explained, "I rather doubt that your friend will crack the password." He confessed that he hadn't, and that he would return them to her.

Peter was wondering if anyone had any suggestions as to why his dogs had scented Hazel on the road. Cricket told him that the Beck girls had seen Hazel and Meredith meeting along that stretch a number of times.

"Maybe it was Mary/Meredith who had walked through the woods on that trail," Peter added.

"She had seemed pretty hardy," I said. "I wonder what Mr. Waverly will tell Lyda about all of this?"

"He's got a lot of explaining to do," Cricket said, "and then they'll probably need to repair some of the damage all those lies caused."

"Speaking of repairs," Jenny said, "we plan on starting renovations next month. Aunt Moira will be a silent partner in the bed and breakfast endeavor, but has promised to visit."

Judd looked around, "It'll be nice."

Peter said, "It'll be work."

We laughed. Judd stood up and said, "I better be off. I've got some shopping to do. It seems the kids changed their minds and are coming up for Christmas."

"That's wonderful," Della said, "Maybe they'd like to stay here. It's all decorated and I'm leaving tomorrow."

He smiled, "That would be real nice."

Everyone was leaving. As Moira stepped off the porch, Cricket reflexively looked at her boot print., "Nope, it wasn't you we chased through the lodge." She was pointing at a boot print in the snow.

Moira laughed, "No it wasn't, but I had you running all over, it was fun. Even the kids from town thought I was an ee-rie spook."

"The blue penlight!" I said, "You used it last night."

Moira laughed louder, "What a bunch of silly kids. Who believes in ghosts anyway?"

I had to give Cricket the *eye of warning* or I'm sure she would have made a fool of herself, or sputtered a hex of sorts. Either one would not have been good.

I offered to close up, Foster helped. As we sat in the quiet, he said, "Now what do we do?"

"I don't know. Holly Fest is over. The will has been found and all of the mysteries are solved. I've even finished my shopping and wrapping."

"Do you want to see if Joe Hill will give us that sleigh ride we missed yesterday?"

I nodded...*to hear sleigh bells in the snow.*

* * *

Driving through town we saw Lyda, Hazel and Meredith Mackenzie Waverly sitting at a window table of the Shipwreck Café.

"I wonder why they didn't invite Trudi." I mused with a giggle.

Foster joined in, "I can't blame them. Maybe she's harassing poor old Elwood."

"I'd like to give Lyda a quick call."

After we hung up I explained to Foster that she and her dad had a long talk. He admitted everything, except making that anonymous phone call to me. It seems that was Vivian."

"Why?" Foster asked.

According to Lyda, Vivian has been devoted to Mr. Waverly for years. She felt sorry for him. She knew about Meredith, too. She was the one snooping around my cabin the night Hazel was presumed lost. She was the elusive snowflake boot print person we'd been looking for. Lyda said she was trying to scare away the True clan. It sounded like Mr. Waverly knew about Vivian's acts of loyalty. She was the only one who knew that he was paying Lyda's mother to stay away. When the money didn't work, he threatened her mother."

"Threatened her with what?" Foster asked.

"Committing her to mental institution, so that she'd never be able to see Lyda."

"That's so sad."

"He claimed he was protecting Lyda by keeping it all secret."

"Protecting himself too, it sounds like. Speaking of secrets," Foster said, "It seems that my aunt has been scheming to get my mom here for Christmas after all."

I'll be home for Christmas...

"That's great. Will her nurse or whoever takes care of her be coming, too?"

"Yep, they have a big van with a wheelchair lift and all the gadgets."

"Whatever happened to her?"

"I don't know. No one will ever talk about it."

We were rounding the corner to Joe Hill Hollow. Snowflakes were gracefully landing on the windshield. I could see the sleigh. Joe was hitching up the team.

"Did you have this all planned?" I asked.

He smiled, "A guy has to have a few secrets of his own. Don't you agree?"

"We all do," I said.

As we climbed onto the snug seat of the sleigh, I tucked my hands into my pockets and thought of how my *gift* was also my curse. Relationships had been a true challenge. I lowered my head as a cold tear slid down my cheek. *If only in my dreams...*

And, so I'm offering this simple phrase...

After we sat quiet for a minute he asked me, "Did you hear Blair call Moira 'cold'?"

I nodded my head, "Sort of, why?"

"Well, after that, Moira said something that caught my attention, like words do sometimes. She said *'Can old lies die?'* Do you see it? It's an acronym, Can Old Lies Die, C-O-.L-D."

"That's interesting, and very fitting of this whole situation, or for anyone. Lies and secrets will make people cold. And it's so *you* to pick up on that."

"Yeah, I know, weird. I just like words."

"I like sleigh rides."

"I know."

He almost tucked his arm around me, but he didn't. Instead we slid quietly through the streets of Ottawa, along forested trails through the Arrowhead Campground by Lake Superior. When we took the road through Joe Hill Hollow we passed Mary Maki's, aka Meredith Mackenzie Waverly's small cabin. I smiled knowing that all of our efforts to preserve our lives gave her back hers.

♦♦ **30** ♦♦

And when the blue heartache starts burning…

As I went home alone that night, I stood for a long moment looking at my little cabin framed by pines with two furry silhouettes perched in the front window. I had so much to be grateful for. Still, a deep sadness tugged at my heart. Maybe it was just the letdown after the party. The holidays can do that.

I forced my feet to follow the moonlit path. As I opened the door, I noticed a light on in the kitchen. There was a clattering of glass.

The kitties jumped to the couch. They weren't acting nervous, so I yelled, "Hello?"

A big round faced poked around the corner of the door, "I was hoping your mom brought you more specials treats!"

I let my breath out in a puff. I hadn't even realized I'd been holding it.

"They're in the refrigerator. There's red velvet with cream cheese frosting."

Cricket squealed and skittered across the kitchen floor.

Within minutes we were sitting on the braided rug, curled in quilts and stuffing red velvet cakes into our mouths. "This is better than sex," Cricket said while licking her fingers, "or at least a close second."

I just answered with a *harrumph*. While contemplating another cake I said, "Now that I know that I'm not going to lose my cabin, and Holly Fest is over, I feel anxious. It's like I need something else to do; something to look forward to."

"Yeah, I've been spending more time away from the shop, too. I feel boxed in once and awhile."

"Della and Jenny have this big new bed and breakfast to work on. Peter will have a project. I feel directionless."

"Lex, you always get like this. You like to help people. It's who you are. You need new projects; Always."

"Is that bad?"

"No; just exhausting."

"I know."

Grabbing the last cake, Cricket said, "You work, I eat; it's how we try to ignore what's going on, or *not going on*, in our lives.

I had to agree, but *the knowing* didn't make me any feel better.

"I was thinking about the business Jenny had worked for in Door County. They make brochures for amusement parks and other small town attractions."

"What brought this about?" Cricket asked as she pulled Pixie onto her lap.

"Well, every time I drive through Ottawa, I think about how we've spruced up the town. Other than relatives and a few snowmobilers, no one knows about it."

"So, you're thinking you'd like to make a brochure about Ottawa?"

"Yeah, maybe that's what I should do."

"Sounds fun. Want help?"

"Sure."

With a sweet sigh, we sat by the fire with Christmas lights twinkling.

"Friends and cake, what more could a girl want."

"Presents?" We laughed, Pixie purred, Pan yowled and the Lake Superior wind whistled,

It's the most wonderful time of the year...